DEAD LOVE HAS CHAINS

MARY ELIZABETH BRADDON

With a new introduction and notes by
LAURENCE TALAIRACH-VIELMAS

VALANCOURT BOOKS

Dead Love Has Chains by Mary Elizabeth Braddon
First published London: Hurst and Blackett, 1907
First Valancourt Books edition 2014

This edition © 2014 by Valancourt Books
Introduction and notes © 2014 by Laurence Talairach-Vielmas

Published by Valancourt Books, Richmond, Virginia
http://www.valancourtbooks.com

ISBN 978-1-939140-20-3 *(trade paper)*
Also available as an electronic book.

All Valancourt Books publications are printed on acid free paper
that meets all ANSI standards for archival quality paper.

Set in Dante MT 11/13.6

CONTENTS

INTRODUCTION

MARY ELIZABETH BRADDON remains famous today for her sensational villainesses, be they murderesses or bigamous women. But Braddon's literary career went far beyond the sensational vogue which took the Victorian reading public by storm in the 1860s. Writing up to two novels a year until her death, with a total of eighty-five novels throughout her literary career, not counting the fiction she wrote anonymously or under a pseudonym for penny and halfpenny journals, the "author of *Lady Audley's Secret*" was above all one of the major figures of Victorian popular fiction. As the editor of two magazines, the *Belgravia* and the *Mistletoe Bough*, a Christmas annual, as a writer of poems, plays, short stories and even fiction for children, Braddon was deeply involved in Victorian literary culture. Often deemed immoral, Braddon's works raised much criticism among those who defended "high literature" and feared the corruptive power of popular literature, however. But whether the hostile attacks of the literary establishment stemmed from the immorality of her fiction or her life, which was as sensational as her fiction—if not more so—is difficult to say.

When her parents separated Mary Elizabeth Braddon was still a child, so her mother, Fanny Braddon—daughter of Patrick White, an Irish Catholic, and Anne Babington, a Protestant—brought up her three children, Maggie, Edward and Mary Elizabeth, alone.[1] When Edward left for India and Maggie married an Italian and settled in Naples in 1847, Mary Elizabeth Braddon remained with her mother, who provided a reasonably good education for her daughter. In 1857 the twenty-two-year-old Braddon, wishing to support the household, went on the stage, under the stage-name

---

1 The materials in this biographical section were taken from Robert Lee Wolff, *Sensational Victorian: The Life and Fiction of Mary Elizabeth Braddon* (New York: Garland Publishing, 1979). See also Jennifer Carnell, *The Literary Lives of Mary Elizabeth Braddon: A Study of Her Life and Work* (Hastings: Sensation Press, 2000).

of "Mary Seyton." In 1860 she swapped her costumes for a pen and published her first novel, *Three Times Dead, or The Secret of the Heath*, later reprinted as *The Trail of the Serpent*. In the same year, she met the publisher John Maxwell with whom she started to live in 1861. Though Maxwell was already married to a woman incarcerated in a lunatic asylum in Dublin, Braddon took care of his five children and bore him six illegitimate children, five of whom survived childhood.

Braddon's fame was sealed with the success of *Lady Audley's Secret*, serialized between 1861-62 in *Robin Goodfellow* and the *Sixpenny Magazine*, and *Aurora Floyd*, the first instalment of which was published in *Temple Bar* before the last instalment of *Lady Audley's Secret*. The former was published as a three-volume novel the following year. By 1866 Braddon had already published nine three-volume novels. She was also editing and contributing to *Belgravia*, which Maxwell had just launched, while continuing to serialize novels elsewhere. In 1867 the deaths of her mother and sister, together with the hostility of the critics, precipitated her nervous collapse, complicated by an attack of puerperal fever. If her production stopped for a year, many other novels followed, her fiction encompassing both the Victorian and Edwardian periods and Braddon still actively writing in her seventies. A typical example is certainly *Dead Love Has Chains*, a novel which, although published in 1907, draws upon the stock conventions of the sensation novels of the 1860s while bringing up themes in keeping with late Victorian and Edwardian preoccupations. Mysteries and double identities are to be found, first lovers or husbands are resurrected and come back to haunt innocent-looking young women, while illnesses are kept secret and the characters' nervous system is constantly placed under scrutiny.

The novel opens with an encounter with a young girl trying to conceal her past. Secrets are hard to keep, it seems, easily leaking out, as when the characters are on board the *Electra* and all windows are open to let air circulate, letting sounds propagate from cabin to cabin. The angelic Irene Thelliston (*alias* Jane Brown) vainly tries to dissimulate her secret, as she leaves Calcutta for Ireland with a broken heart. As usual with Braddon Irene's languid sensuality, evincing her fallenness, evokes Victorian paintings of voluptuous female characters, such as the exhausted female characters draped in folds of cloth in Alfred Moore's, Frederic Leighton's or Lawrence Alma-Tadema's works—painters mentioned later on whose works decorate Lady Harling's house. Visual references thus discreetly frame the first depiction of the young woman loosely wrapped in a white dressing-gown with bare feet in red slippers while allusions to Pre-Raphaelite stunners also appear later on to define female beauty. But the popular clichés Braddon draws on fabricate an ambivalent vision of the female character: oscillating as she does between sensuous fleshliness and "ethereality," Irene is as ambiguous as the sensational villainesses and heroines which made Braddon's fame. For the novel recurrently suggests that women are actresses, works of art or "mock angels": their beauty is made up, they consult beauty-specialists, resort to surgery, have their faces flayed, some of the characters' complexion coming "out of bottles" (65). The artificial construction of the feminine ideal is therefore presented as common practice, even if female characters like Stella, whose virginal innocence, blue eyes, golden lashes and flaxen hair fashion her into a double of Lucy Audley for readers well-versed in sensation fiction, are at the root of evil. Women's deceitfulness, women's secrets, or women's sexual life drive the plot, Braddon even playing upon female doubles, such as Stella and Irene, both in love with Conrad, both shaken by "convulsive sobbing" (14) or "stormy sobs that threatened hysteria" (30) and both deserting him.

Compared to earlier sensation novels, the plot of *Dead Love Has Chains* proceeds in reverse, however, the narrative using flashbacks and thus playing more upon dramatic irony than suspense. Because of the narrative structure, indeed, the reader suspects that Jane Brown and Irene Thelliston are one and the same long before the revelation: Lady Harling's second encounter with the young woman becomes anti-climactic, weighing the narrative with a sense of impending doom, recurrently recalled by allusions to Shakespeare's tragedy *Romeo and Juliet*. Moreover, if, as Irene says, "there is no pardon for a woman's sin" (80), Braddon's denunciation of the Victorian and Edwardian double standard permeates the novel and foreshadows the unravelling of the narrative. Her female characters are doomed to sin, it appears, even if the motif of the double functions as a red herring since Irene is eventually cast into the role of the victim at the end of the novel. In addition, Braddon time and again contrasts male and female characters, hinging her portraits upon biological constructions of gender differences and presenting characters subjected to unruly physiologies.

If Robert Audley seemed to be driven by providence in *Lady Audley's Secret*, the fate that threatens the main character reveals rather Braddon's French literary influences. As a matter of fact, *Dead Love Has Chains* illustrates Braddon's capacity to adapt her fiction to her public and remain up to date, especially regarding the latest conceptions of the brain, revamping her earlier portraits of insane women. In 1867, Braddon had been accused of plagiarism after the publication of *Circe*, a rewriting of the Frenchman Octave Feuillet's play, *Dalila* (1857). What the accusation exposed, above all, was that Braddon was well read in French literature. She travelled extensively throughout her life, could read and write in French, had a subscription to the French circulating library Rolandi in London, read French journals, such as the *Revue des Deux Mondes*, and loved French literature from Balzac and Zola to Flaubert, Maupassant or Dumas. The names of such French writers often figure in her fiction as tell-tale devices, giving her characters a fragrance of licentiousness, immorality or flightiness. In *Dead Love Has Chains*, French words are found very regularly and the reading of French novels is associated with idleness, breeding young girls' depravity, just as it typified Robert Audley's lack of will-power half a century before. Balzac, in particular, appeared in several of Braddon's novels, such as *Birds of Prey* (1867) and its sequel, *Charlotte's Inheritance* (1868), in which a poisoner reads Balzac, while her 1891 novel *Gerard* is based upon Balzac's *La Peau de chagrin* (1831). Yet, in addition to functioning as hints at perversion or degeneracy, the influence of French literature, especially in her novels of the 1880s, showed Braddon's interest in naturalism. The recurrent theme of alcohol and the figures of drunkards, as in *The Cloven Foot* (1879), in which a French ballet-dancer takes to drink, or *The Golden Calf* (1883), in which the drinking and smoking male protagonist becomes paranoid and deluded, are so many examples of Braddon's reliance on naturalistic themes and motifs. Shifting from Balzac and Flaubert (as exemplified by *The Doctor's Wife*, a reworking of Flaubert's *Madame Bovary*), to Zolaesque characters, Braddon followed the literary trends of the era, adapting French characters to English society and often featuring degenerate English gentlemen. Her growing interest in the theory of heredity to explain her characters' behavioural instincts radically differed from her first use of heredity as a means of escaping a murder sentence, as in her seminal sensation novel *Lady Audley's Secret*. By the 1880s, her Zolaesque characters had gained in psychological depth. The use of the heredity motif, moreover, illustrated in *The Golden Calf* (1883), *Phantom Fortune* (1883) or *Ishmael* (1884), also gave Braddon a chance to display her talent for realistic delineations of medical cases. This is most evident in *The Golden Calf*, in which Braddon describes the male protagonist's degeneration and his gradual descent into *delirium tremens*, developing a theme she had already raised in *Eleanor's Victory* (1863), in *Thou Art the Man*, in which the male protagonist suffers from hereditary epilepsy and eventually becomes mad, and in *Dead Love Has Chains*, in which the hero is found mad after a nervous breakdown and has to go into a nursing home.

Dead Love Has Chains is, indeed, focused on Conrad Harling's "love-madness" (40) or "melancholy madness" (41). Conrad Harling is "a romantic young man, full of high-flown sentiments and wild Quixotism" (25) with Republican views. But his "impassioned" (28), or "highly emotional temperament" (45) makes him vulnerable to mental disease. Hence his collapse when he finds himself deserted by his *fiancée*. Mad male characters were not germane to Braddon's novels and appeared as early as in the 1860s. This is notably the case of the short story "The Mystery at Fernwood" published in *Temple Bar* in 1861, a rewriting of Charlotte Brontë's *Jane Eyre* (1847).[1] While the short story evinced the influence of

---

1 Mary Elizabeth Braddon, "The Mystery at Fernwood," *Temple Bar* 3 (Nov. 1861): 552-563; 4 (March 1862): 63-74.

Jane Eyre upon Braddon's writing,[1] it illuminated as well Braddon's fascination with madness and the ways in which her depictions of mentally ill characters matched contemporary definitions of insanity. At mid-century, Charlotte Brontë's description of the mad Bertha Mason was in line with current medical thinking about mental pathologies. Suffering from "moral insanity," as defined by Esquirol's treatise on insanity, *Des Maladies mentales* (1838),[2] and popularised by J. C. Pritchard's *Treatise on Insanity* in England,[3] Bertha is considered as morally corrupted, her species of insanity being therefore linked with her immoral behaviour. The use of insanity is similar in *Lady Audley's Secret*, since the villainess "has the cunning of madness, with the prudence of intelligence,"[4] her mental derangement being associated with no lesion of the intellect but resulting rather from her sinful deeds. However, images of female insanity in Brontë's novel, and more strikingly in the sensation novels of the 1860s, were used above all to encode complaints about women's condition and oppression in a patriarchal society and denounce the limited choices offered to Victorian women outside marriage.

As Helen Small has shown, the madwomen who appeared in sensation novels of the 1860s were inspired by late eighteenth- and early nineteenth-century sentimental stereotypical images of female insanity, such as those of women going mad when they lose their lovers, extolled by novelists, dramatists, poets or painters

1 Many of Braddon's works refer to *Jane Eyre*. "The Mystery at Fernwood" relates the story of two twin-brothers, one of whom is insane and locked up on the top floor of Fernwood. His insanity results from a fall which caused a fatal injury to the brain. In "The Flight from Wealdon Hall," Braddon has the governess help the mad wife to escape. Braddon even wrote an essay on Charlotte Brontë, published as "At the Shrine of 'Jane Eyre'," *Pall Mall Magazine* 37 (1906) : 174-176.

2 Jean-Etienne Dominique Esquirol, *Des Maladies mentales* (Paris, 1838), translated as *Mental Maladies: A Treatise on Insanity*, translated with additions by E. K. Hunt (London, 1845).

3 Helen Small, *Love's Madness: Medicine, the Novel, and Female Insanity, 1800-1865* (Oxford: Clarendon Press, 1996), 163. For more on Bertha Mason and "moral insanity" see Philip Martin, *Mad Women in Romantic Writing* (New York: St. Martin's Press, 1987), 124-139.

4 Mary Elizabeth Braddon, *Lady Audley's Secret* [1862] (Oxford: Oxford University Press, 1987), 379.

during the cult of sensibility.[1] The character of Lucy Audley, for instance, is a modern rewriting of Ophelia, Lady Audley's mental disturbance starting after her husband's desertion, even if the patient is allegedly plagued with hereditary insanity. Furthermore, seminal sensation novels were also deeply ingrained in a period which saw major reform initiatives in the history of insanity. Wilkie Collins's *The Woman in White* was serialized in November 1859, just a few months after two major "lunacy panics" in Britain: the revelation of wrongful confinement of sane men and women led to the establishment of a Select Committee of Inquiry, represented by the Alleged Lunatics' Friend Society.[2] In addition, the serialization of *The Woman in White* corresponded with the publication and widespread discussion of the Parliamentary Select Committee Inquiry into the Care and Treatment of Lunatics and Their Property of 1858-59.[3] Wilkie Collins was a known supporter of the asylum reform movement and close to the significant figures connected with psychological medicine, such as Bryan Procter (1787-1874), who was a Lunacy Commissioner between 1832 and 1861 and was the dedicatee of *The Woman in White*, just like Charles Dickens, whose villainess, Miss Havisham, in *Great Expectations* (1861), may be seen as a double of Collins's woman in white. Charles Reade, another famous writer associated with the sensation genre, was also involved in lunacy reform, his *Hard Cash* (1863) featuring a parody of John Conolly (1794-1866), an alienist much involved in new methods for dealing with the insane in mental homes and who denounced wrongful confinements in private madhouses. In 1865 the establishment of the Medico-Psychological Association (later to become the Royal College of Psychiatrists) was another landmark underlining the links between the sensational madwomen that were captivating the Victorians at the time and the history of insanity. It was also in 1859-60 that Henry Maudsley—Conolly's son-in-law—published his views on hereditary insanity for the first time.

---

1 Small, *Love's Madness.*

2 See Small, *Love's Madness*, for more on the links between sensational madwomen and the history of insanity.

3 Jenny Bourne Taylor, *In the Secret Theatre of Home: Wilkie Collins, Sensation Narrative and Nineteenth Century Psychology* (London: Routledge, 1988), 30.

The more humanistic treatment of the insane that emerged in the first half of the nineteenth century is, indeed, recurrently alluded to in many sensation novels. The private asylums that appear in *Lady Audley's Secret*, Reade's *Hard Cash*, Collins's *The Woman in White*, *Armadale* (1864) and *The Law and the Lady* (1875), or the references to Bedlam in Collins's *Jezebel's Daughter* (1880), are so many examples typifying the links between the rise and development of sensation fiction and the movement of public contestation surrounding the treatment of the insane—a link that went far beyond the 1860s. Multiple references may be traced to the development of techniques of "moral management" as a new way of treating insanity, for instance, freeing the insane from their chains and cages, as Pinel did in Paris or William Tuke (1732-1822) in England at the turn of the nineteenth century. The bestial insane, just like the brutal methods to treat them, gradually vanished from popular representations, as alienists like Conolly helped the opening of madhouses (such as the Middlesex County Asylum at Hanwell) supporting non-restraint management.[1] Like *Lady Audley's Secret* half a century before, *Dead Love Has Chains* illustrates Braddon's interest in definitions and classifications of madness as well as her concern with the care of the insane. The madman's mother's first preoccupation is that her son "should never know the restraints that other mental sufferers know" (40). If Conrad is nonetheless sent to a private asylum, he is well looked after, well fed, invited to read, play tennis or croquet: "the system and details were the highest outcome of modern science and modern thought. Nowhere could this martyr of a foolish love-dream be better cared for" (41). The methods of moral management are applied ("Proper exercise had been insisted upon, slouching habits had been prevented" (45)), encouraging the mentally ill to develop self-regulation and control his will. For the will, as the novel illuminates, was indeed at the basis of mid-nineteenth-century mental physiologists' or alienists' definitions of the

---

1 Pinel's "moral treatment" was advocated by Esquirol in France, W.A.F. Browne (*What Asylums Were, Are, and Ought to Be* (1837)), John Conolly (*The Treatment of the Insane Without Mechanical Restraints* (1856)) or Forbes Winslow (*On Obscure Diseases of the Brain and Disorders of the Mind* (1860)) in England, all inviting their patients to develop self-regulation.

mind. As George Henry Lewes, alongside many other nineteenth-century psychologists believed, the will was "educatable, and . . . amenable to the Moral law."¹ This is why, after the second shock, Conrad, now aware of his susceptibility to mental illness, has also learnt to control his will: as he walks in a "semiconscious state," his "[m]emory [...] shaken [having] lost count of time" (129), he nonetheless manages to regain his mental balance by counting the vehicles and naming them.

Unlike men, however, women's supposed weak will, which inevitably constructed women as typical nervous sufferers and placed them alongside animals and half-wits on the evolutionary scale, explains why insanity became "an extension of [the] female condition"² in many sensation novels of the 1860s. Because it matched contemporary constructions of femininity, defining women as weak and liable to suffer from debility of the nerves, Victorian madwomen embodied a typically feminine condition whether they suffered from simple nervous exhaustion, hysteria or even mania. But Braddon's twist to the eighteenth-century sentimental icon of the love-mad woman indicates how Victorian popular fiction could turn hackneyed clichés on their heads. If, as suggested, Lucy Audley was inspired by the literary convention of the Ophelian madwoman, she no longer embodies ideals of sensibility: Braddon's reliance upon theories of hereditary insanity connects the character's mental disturbance to the workings of the body. Braddon's sensational revision of the trope of the madwoman, as one of the many metaphors that define the feminine ideal, shows how the reworking of such sentimental icons by sensation writers in the 1860s and their recurrent play upon the gendering of madness as a female condition was a direct response to the medical discourses that confined women within subordinate positions through defining them as weak and passive beings. The weight of medical discourse that permeates sensation novels points out the genre's denunciation of the authority of medical science and its infiltration into the social sphere. Moreover, by choosing a male character to play the part

1 George Henry Lewes, *Problems of Life and Mind, Problem the First: The Study of Psychology, Its Object, Scope and Method* (London: Trübner & Co., 1879), 109.
2 Small, *Love's Madness*, viii.

of the Ophelian madwoman in *Dead Love Has Chains* Braddon deliberately undermined dominant Victorian gender representations, even if, as shall be seen, her choice illuminates changing visions of insanity at the turn of the twentieth century.

Of course, the novel does play upon the excitability of women and emphasizes their liability to suffer from nervous ailments. The first chapter of the novel deals with women's health and emotions. It opens on reflections on chronic illnesses, linking them with idleness, foreshadowing the depiction of the heart-broken Irene Thelliston (*alias* Jane Brown), whose crying and "hysterical" (4) behaviour betrays her sexual secret. The fallen woman is first and foremost introduced through her unbalanced nervous system, her lack of will-power, evidenced by her loose clothes, her lethargy due to over-excitement while her excitability is strengthened by the novels she chooses in Lady Harling's library: Charlotte Brontë's *Jane Eyre* and Nathaniel Hawthorne's *The Scarlet Letter.* If the intertextual references function as clues, hinting at Irene's secret, her selection also betrays her sexual appetite. The idea that reading was linked with physical appetite and had to be controlled, especially for young and emotionally susceptible women prevailed all through the nineteenth century. The fear that some reading might affect women more than men followed the developments in mental physiology and their definitions of the interrelations between the mind and the body—or the "brain and the heart," as some psychologists contended.[1] Women's vulnerability and susceptibility to emotions explains why types and modes of reading were surveyed. Braddon's awareness of current debates on women's reading (which were particularly striking when the sensation novel was raging) informs the novel. Lady Harling's reading of sermons, for instance, meant to strengthen her mind, or Conrad's reading of poetry, fiction, history or science as a cure to his madness, are stereotypical, while Irene, who reads improper novels overnight, such as Hawthorne's *The Scarlet Letter,* and takes Henry Middlemore for "the typical Guardsman of the romantic novel" (96), is

---

1 George Henry Lewes, "The Heart and the Brain," *The Fortnightly Review* 1 (15 May 1865): 66-74.

more likely to be vulnerable to the power of novels to corrupt the mind. Thus, the many literary references that pepper the narrative, if they call upon the reader's literary knowledge and participate in the construction of suspense,[1] are in line with nineteenth-century modes of reading and highlight the influence of mental physiology on gender constructions.

Moreover, the characters' physiology plays a key part in the narrative. The very first lines of the novel concern Lady Harling's chronic illness and the cures that inefficient physicians devise for her, sending her to various parts of the world. Interestingly, Miss Brown is first introduced as "too ill or too unhappy to appear in public" (4), and the opening chapter constantly aligns her "overstrung nerves" (8) with her "broken" heart (14). We may here remember Charles Dickens's Miss Havisham in 1861, whose mechanical appearance and hysteria were related to her "broken heart" as well. Dickens's, just like Braddon's hysterical characters, map out the gradual rationalization and scientific framing of the heart in the second half of the nineteenth century. Their madwomen show how the seat of emotions changed throughout the nineteenth century, as neuro-physiology gradually placed the mind at the heart of emotions. As emotions were redefined by physiologists "as a product of sensory perception and material processes,"[2] physiological research paved the way for the shift from cardio-centric to neuro-centric understandings of emotional experiences. With the development of neuro-physiology, therefore, emotions were more and more linked to brain mechanisms. The replacement of the heart by the brain as the organ linked with emotions is manifest in many portraits of Ophelian-like Victorian madwomen. But late Victorian popular fiction also revealed how the changing of the roles of the heart and the brain were linked to the development of pathological anatomy, to research into cere-

1 Braddon's fiction generally contains many literary references, Shakespeare appearing perhaps most frequently. *The Doctor's Wife*, a rewriting of Flaubert's *Madame Bovary* (1857), epitomizes more than any other novel Braddon's reliance upon intertextual vignettes.
2 Fay Bound Alberti, *Matters of the Heart: History, Medicine and Emotion* (Oxford: Oxford University Press, 2010), 29.

bral localization and studies in craniology and phrenology, most notably through manifold references to the famous physiologists of the second part of the nineteenth century, from John Hughlings Jackson (1835-1911) to David Ferrier (1843-1928), for instance. Braddon's focus on the hearts and brains of her characters and the connections between body and mind shows, indeed, that *Dead Love Has Chains* is in keeping with *fin-de-siècle* preoccupations in its treatment of mental illnesses. The description of Conrad's nervous breakdown could be compared to Bram Stoker's *Dracula* (1897), a novel which explores research into the understanding and mapping of the brain and directly cites figures like John Scott Burdon-Sanderson (1828-1905) or Ferrier. At the beginning of the novel Mina Harker, worried about her husband's health, consults Dr. Van Helsing because her *fiancé*, Jonathan Harker, had "a sort of shock"[1] in the Carpathians, followed by a brain fever. Although the doctor believes that Harker's constitution makes him a patient not likely "to be injured in permanence by a shock" and contends that his "brain and heart are all right,"[2] his medical verdict foregrounds the novel's concern with late nineteenth-century investigations of the brain. Throughout the narrative, the medical professionals investigate the origins of brain disease, aligning the heart and the brain in their explanations of their patients' illnesses. Suffering from vampirism, the characters—Jonathan Harker and Lucy Westenra—become hypersensitive and exhibit symptoms very close to the alienist's (Dr. Seward) patient, Renfield. Heartbreaks are defined as "wounds" which refuse to "becom[e] cicatrized"[3] and reopen, drawing comparisons with the vampire's bites—small punctured wounds on the victims' throats—while emotions are represented as blood being "drain[ed] to the head,"[4] as when the poor emaciated Lucy turns crimson at the remembrance of Dr. Seward's marriage proposal. The debate between the heart and the brain which *Dracula* point to is a long one, but the *fin-de-siècle*

---

1 Bram Stoker, *Dracula* [1897], edited by Nina Auerbach & David S. Skal (New York: Norton & Company, 1997), 165.
2 Stoker, *Dracula*, 167.
3 Stoker, *Dracula*, 170.
4 Stoker, *Dracula*, 120.

novel, figuring medical practitioners holding post-mortem knives to remove young women's hearts and alienists dreaming about carrying out vivisection on human beings to advance the knowledge of the brain, illustrates the medicalization of emotions and the secularization of psychology that the novel draws upon in its revision of the vampire myth.

Likewise, Braddon's *Dead Love Has Chains* hinges upon contemporary constructions of mental diseases, resorting as well to the image of the "wound" in the hero's mind which prevents Conrad from mastering his own self: Conrad is sent to a private asylum "till the wound in that beautiful mind [is] healed, and he [is] again a free man and master of his life" (40). Braddon's choice of a mad male character whose pathology matches current constructions of mental disturbances, as in *The Golden Calf* or *Thou Art the Man*, marks the popular writer's move away from the sensational characters and plots that had made her fame half a century before. For as argued, if women were defined as nervously debilitated, men were, on the contrary, supposed to incarnate the bourgeois ideal of manliness that implied mental and physical strength—an ideal which was reinforced in late Victorian imperialist fiction, notably by writers of adventure fiction for boys in the last decades of the nineteenth century.

Many of Braddon's novels showed her awareness of and interest in the empire. References to India and the Indian Mutiny may be found in *Lady Audley's Secret*,[1] while *Thou Art the Man* is set in 1886, recalling the political unrest in South Africa following the Cape Frontier or Kaffir wars (1779-1879), the Anglo-Zulu War (1879) and the first Boer war (1880-81), and *Dead Love Has Chains* possibly alludes to the Benin expedition of 1897, the third Anglo-Burmese war of 1885 and British expeditions in Waziristan at the turn of the century. In addition, her late Victorian novels frequently pivot upon the issues of "barbarism" and "civilization" or the fear of degeneration, themes which fuelled the literature of the period,

---

1 See Lilian Nayder, "Rebellious Sepoys and Bigamous Wives: The Indian Mutiny and Marriage Law Reform in *Lady Audley's Secret*," in Marlene Tromp, Pamela K. Gilbert and Aeron Haynie (eds), *Beyond Sensation: Mary Elizabeth Braddon in Context* (Albany: State University of New York Press, 2000), 31-42.

particularly marked by the publication of Rider Haggard's imperialist fiction: *King's Solomon's Mines* (1885), *She: A History of Adventure* (1887), and *Allan Quatermain* (1887). In the vein of Captain
Richard Burton's and other contemporary explorers' narratives,
Haggard—who had spent five years in South Africa, like Braddon's male character in *Thou Art the Man*—featured the unknown
Dark Continent as a territory to be "explored and conquered," in
Rebecca Stott's words.[1] In his novels, the male characters go on a
quest, penetrating and investigating the mysterious Dark Continent to discover the dangerous female criminal at the heart of the
story and the dangers of female sexuality. The conflation of woman
and Africa underlay much imperialist fiction of the late nineteenth
century which often shaped the male quest as an anthropological
hunt, describing explorers in search of the stigmata of atavism on
the unmapped body of Africa/woman.[2] Thus, as anthropological
science was focusing on the criminal's cranium and used woman's
stunted brain-size as evidence of woman's atavistic features, the
anthropological romances of the 1880s featured male explorers
searching for the very signs by which to read the dark woman as
an evolutionary throwback.

Braddon had undoubtedly read Haggard's novels. Haggard
had a publishing contract with John (known as Jack) and Robert
Maxwell, and novels such as *Thou Art the Man* suggest that Braddon
revisited Haggard's imperialist romances of the 1880s, reworking
in particular the figure of the male explorer by turning him into an
evolutionary throwback. Likewise, in *Dead Love Has Chains* nonfic-
tional imperial quest romances are mentioned: Conrad reads and
recites anecdotes from Verney Lovett Cameron's (1844-1894) *Across
Africa* (1877) and Henry Morton Stanley's (1844-1904) *How I Found
Livingstone* (1872). But Braddon's mad male character turns the
male plot of imperialist romance on its head: Central Africa serves
to conceal the fact that Conrad is locked away in a private asylum.
In ways similar to *Thou Art the Man*, therefore, the comparison
between Africa and the mental home collapses the portrait of the

---

1 Rebecca Stott, *The Fabrication of the Late Victorian Femme Fatale: The Kiss of
Death* (London: Macmillan, 1992), 93.
2 See Stott, *The Fabrication of the Late Victorian Femme Fatale*, 88-125.

manful British "civilized" explorer. Although Braddon foregrounds
both her characters' "unusual strength of will and unusual sensitiveness" (63), the male patient subverts gender constructions: his
illness constantly threatens the ideal of manliness, since mental
strength and emotional control were believed to march hand in
hand with physical strength. As Conrad's rivals suggest, indeed,
sheer physical force encapsulates the male ideal. Stella runs away
with "an olive-skinned gladiator" whose "muscular arms" and
"brute force" (35) seduce the young woman, while Henry Middlemore is tall, "broad and stalwart" (116) with strong arms, a "coarse
brute—a creature of thews and sinews" (125). Irene's father
can also boast a military career, "fighting all his life—in India—
Egypt—Africa—always doing well" (62). Not contributing much
to his nation's economy, unlike his father who was a shipbuilder,
Conrad seems at odds in an industrial world, as if bearing the
seeds of his mother's ancient family. To a certain extent, Conrad's
emotional sensitivity aligns him with earlier sensational male characters, such as Walter Hartright in *The Woman in White*, who leaves
for South America and comes back physically and mental stronger,
or Ovid Vere in *Heart and Science* who recovers in Canada.[1] Such
examples illuminate how male nervous disorders jarred at a time
of industrial and imperialist expansion as the many references to
Asia and Africa suggest throughout the novel.

But Braddon also brings mental diseases up to date with a *fin-
de-siècle* context. It is true that many details draw links between
Conrad and earlier models of insane male characters. Allusions
to Dickens's Manette in *A Tale of Two Cities* (1859) may be traced
as Conrad is described in his "house of bondage" (45), recalling
Dickens's character locked up in his tower, both being character-
ized by their mechanical appearance or the description of their
"bodily machine[s]" (45) working. But the rarity of Conrad's case
is also underlined, for his mental derangement results above all
from an emotional shock which has provoked physical lesions in
the brain. Indeed, unlike William Wendale in "The Mystery at

---

1 See Jane Wood, *Passion and Pathology in Victorian Fiction* (Oxford: Oxford University Press, 2001), 75.

Fernwood," whose fall causes a fatal injury to the brain, Conrad's form of insanity is linked with his psychological trauma after being deserted—the description of his trauma matching late nineteenth-century views of the effects of shock. Especially spurred by the railway disasters of the 1850s and 1860s, the medical discourse of shock developed in England in the second half of the nineteenth century, as British psychophysiology more and more saw emotions as bodily and physical and resulting from a physiological process.[1] Many sensation novels, aimed at thrilling their readers, touched upon emotions and even trauma—we may here mention Laura Fairlie's traumatic experience in the lunatic asylum in *The Woman in White*, manifest in the way in which her stay in the asylum affects her memory. This is even more stressed in *Dead Love Has Chains* since the idea of trauma surges whenever the character's altered states of consciousness (or his "slumber" (47, 56)) are combined with memory losses. As in *The Fatal Three* and *Thou Art the Man*, madness is seen as "the sudden extinction of thought and memory" (49), and the character's recovery is gauged through his strengthening memory. At the same time, the time line of the narrative, punctuated by flashbacks and denying chronology, seems to metaphorically mimic the character's efforts at training his memory not to drift into madness. Eventually, Conrad not only exercises his will, but his cure consists as well in getting physically involved in his expanding empire and leaving for Africa to "do something that would call upon his thews and sinews, and give his brain a holiday (131). As usual with Braddon the closure of the story seems to reinforce dominant constructions, making her novels highly significant examples of Victorian and Edwardian popular fiction. However, her play with literary conventions and the relationship between gender constructs and medical discourse that she generally develops in her novels also show how popular writers participated in debates about health and disease and alerted the reading public as to the authority of medical science and its impact upon other areas and discourses. In *Dead Love Has Chains*, in particular,

1 Jill Matus, "Emergent Theories of Victorian Mind Shock: From War and Railway Accident to Nerves, Electricity and Emotion," in Anne Stiles (ed.), *Neurology and Literature, 1860-1920* (Houndmills: Palgrave Macmillan, 2007), 163-183, 169.

the portrait of an insane and hypersensitive man in a masculinist culture enables Braddon to offer a more sympathetic approach to nervously susceptible men which typifies the role that popular writers played to negotiate tensions and challenge the very stereotypes which informed their works.

LAURENCE TALAIRACH-VIELMAS
Toulouse

October 24, 2013

A CHRONOLOGY OF MARY ELIZABETH BRADDON

1835   Born 4 October, 2 Frith Street, Soho Square.

1847   Her brother Edward goes to India; her sister Maggie marries an Italian and goes to Naples to live. M. E. Braddon stays alone with her mother.

1857-60 Goes on the stage as "Mary Seyton."

1860   Publishes her first novel, *Three Times Dead, or The Secret of the Heath*, reissued in 1861 as *The Trail of the Serpent*.

1861   Starts her liaison with the publisher John Maxwell, whose wife was incarcerated in a lunatic asylum in Dublin. Maxwell launches *The Halfpenny Journal*, a weekly periodical to which she contributes several novels anonymously (*The Black Band; or The Mysteries of Midnight*, *The Octoroon; or The Lily of Louisiana*; *Captain of the Vulture*; *A Romance of Real Life*).

1861   *The Lady Lisle.*

1862   *Lady Audley's Secret.*

1863   *Aurora Floyd; Eleanor's Victory; John Marchmont's Legacy.* Writes *The White Phantom* and *The Factory Girl; or, All Is Not Gold That Glitters; Oscar Bertrand; or The Idiot of the Mountain* for *The Halfpenny Journal*.

1864   *Henry Dunbar; The Doctor's Wife.*

1865   *Only a Clod; Sir Jasper's Tenant.* Writes *The Banker's Secret* for *The Halfpenny Journal*.

1866   *The Lady's Mile.* Maxwell sells *Temple Bar* and founds the monthly *Belgravia*. M. E. Braddon becomes the editor and publishes under the pseudonym of "Babington White." Braddon purchases Lichfield House in Richmond where she would live with Maxwell and her children for the rest of their lives.

1867   Publishes *Circe* in *Belgravia* under the pseudonym of "Babington White." Accused of plagiarism. *Rupert Godwin*, a rewriting of *The Banker's Secret* as a three-volume novel.

1867-68 *Birds of Prey* and its sequel *Charlotte's Inheritance; Dead Sea Fruit.*

1868   Death of mother and sister. Nervous collapse and attack of puerperal fever.

1870   *Milly Darrell.*

1871   *Fenton's Quest; The Lovels of Arden.*

1872   *To the Bitter End.*

1873   *Lucius Davoren; Strangers and Pilgrims.*

1874   Death of John Maxwell's wife. Marries Maxwell on 2 October. *Taken at the Flood; Lost For Love.*

1875   *A Strange World; Hostages to Fortune; Dead Men's Shoes.*

1876   *Belgravia* sold to Chatto and Windus. Braddon ceases to be its editor. *Joshua Haggard's Daughter.*

1877   *Weavers and Weft.*

1878   *An Open Verdict.* Founds *The Mistletoe Bough*, a new Christmas annual to which she contributes several novels and novelettes, such as *Flower and Weed* (1882) and *Under the Red Flag* (1883).

1879   *Vixen; The Cloven Foot.*

1880   *The Story of Barbara; Just As I Am.*

1881   *Asphodel.*

1882   *Mount Royal.* Writes plays (*Married Beneath Him; Dross; Margery Daw*).

1883   *The Golden Calf; Phantom Fortune.*

1884   *Ishmael.*

1885   *Wyllard's Weird.*

1886   *Mohawks; One Thing Needful.*

1887   *Like and Unlike.*

1888   *The Fatal Three.*

1889   *The Day Will Come.*

1890   *One Life One Love.*

1891   *Gerard.*

1892   *The Venetians.*

1892-93 *The Christmas Hirelings*, a Christmas novelette.

1893   *All Along the River.*

1894   *Thou Art the Man* published in three volumes (London: Simpkin, Marshall) after having run serially in Leng's *Sheffield Weekly Telegraph*.

1895   Death of John Maxwell. *Sons of Fire*, last three-volume novel.

1896   *London Pride.*

1897   *Under Love's Rule.*

1898   *Rough Justice; In High Places.*

1899   Daughter Rosie (Lachlan) dies. *His Darling Sin.*

1900   *The Infidel.*

1903   *The Conflict.*

1904   Death of brother. *A Lost Eden.*

1905   *The Rose of Life.*

DEAD LOVE HAS CHAINS

CHAPTER I

LADY MARY HARLING was going back to England, after a winter in Ceylon. She was too idle, too utterly without ambitions or views, to be free from chronic illness. She suffered from a tendency to asthma, in a very mild form, always talked of by herself and her friends as her asthma; as if it were a rare and peculiar malady, while there were dressmakers' assistants and factory girls in London reckoned by thousands, who were afflicted in the same manner, and who took the thing as a matter of course, just an occasional shortness of breath that made hard work and long hours a shade more irksome. In Whitechapel* and Bermondsey* it was everybody's asthma, occasioning frequent visits to the Dispensary; in Hertford Street, Mayfair,* it was Lady Mary Harling's asthma, and a theme for fashionable physicians to expatiate upon with unctuous solicitude, meditating, or seeming to meditate, profoundly, before they advised the precise spot upon this globe that would be best for their cherished patient in the coming winter. Last year it had been Assouan, and the year before it had been Cairo, and the year before that St. Moritz, and before that Meran. This last winter had been spent in Ceylon; and Lady Mary was going home bored to death with all that she had seen and done, the gardens, temples, palaces, bazaars, people—most of all the white people she knew in England. She was going home, not happy, but resigned, knowing that there was more boredom waiting for her—the impalpable invisible black devil of ennui in town and country, in her too spacious house in Hertford Street, in her fine old Georgian mansion in Hampshire, on the edge of the New Forest.

Needless to say that Lady Mary had one of the best cabins, midship, on the upper deck of the *Electra*, one of the finest steamers recently built by the most renowned company trafficking in passengers only between the Thames and the Hoogly. It was a cabin for three, adapted for one, and in a smaller cabin on the same expensive deck she had her maid and her *souffre-douleur,** a dowerless kinswoman of six-and-twenty, whom she had taken to herself eight years before, when the girl was young and pretty, and when her friends hoped that in such distinguished surroundings she might make a comfortable, or even a brilliant marriage. The poor child's chances in the matrimonial line were blighted by a terrible sorrow that came upon Lady Mary in the second year of Daisy Meredith's service, a calamity that put a sudden end to all foregatherings of the young and lively in Hertford Street, or at Cranford Park. As years wore on Lady Mary had seen more society, but she seemed to have taken an aversion to young people, and never had any of them about her.

"I can't amuse them, and they don't amuse me," she said, when her intimates accused her of cultivating dulness.

She let the Cranford shooting, and gave the money to a Bournemouth hospital. Her friends were all of them past forty, some grave and learned, some frivolous and pleasure-loving, but none young. From young men in particular she shrank with a kind of disgust. She could better put up with girls. This was a consequence of the great grief that had come upon her suddenly when Daisy Meredith was nineteen.

Daisy at twenty-six had made up her mind to a life of spinsterhood, and did not even know that she was still pretty. She was attached to her friend and protectress, who had taken her from a shabby home in an interminable road in the dismal north of London, and from her place as buffer between a father and mother who quarrelled incessantly when they were together, and who occasionally separated, but always made the mistake of coming together again. The life in Hertford Street was elysium after the life in the Seven Sisters' Road; and Daisy was able to be of more use to her mother by little gifts out of her handsome allowance than ever she had been as buffer. The allowance was called pocket-money, and everybody knew her as a useful cousin, and not a salaried companion.

Somewhere in the hull of the ship there was a footman, whose most arduous duties during the voyage were limited to the careful placing of her ladyship's deck-chair, rugs, and sun-umbrellas, on the promenade deck, generally wrong as to wind and sun till corrected by one of the ship's officers, and in fetching and carrying books and magazines and work bags at Miss Meredith's bidding. Like most women of large means and no ambitions, Lady Mary was an accomplished needle-woman, deeply interested in every revival of old art in pictorial embroidery. Her latest task was a panel for a screen, a landscape of Dutch formality, with a row of poplars in a laborious raised stitch, every tree requiring months of patient toil. The panel, closely veiled in tissue paper, was stretched on a frame, and to establish this conveniently for Lady Mary's labour was a work of time. It gave the cousin and maid and footman something to do every morning, either on the open deck or in the ladies' drawing-room, and to re-establish it in her ladyship's cabin after luncheon.

Lady Mary had acknowledged to eight-and-forty for the last three years, but was believed, from the evidence of history, to be older. She had been seventeen years a widow, and was still handsome enough to bring no shame upon handsome clothes. Dress was a subject to which she gave serious thought, and she considered herself successful. She loved bright colour; in her houses, and in her gowns.

"I had rather be garish than dull," she told people.

That great sorrow, the unutterable grief of six years ago, had spread so dark a pall over the life of the heart, that she had been forced to take pleasure in externals.

"I have only things to interest me," she said. "I am always bored, but I make a good fight against boredom."

She was a member of the Dante Society, and took a keen delight in their proceedings, and read a little Dante every day as piously as her Bible. She took Daisy Meredith to all the best concerts of the season, to hear all the old favourites, and all the new prodigies on piano or fiddle.

"It is good for you, if it sometimes bores me," she said.

So it will be seen that Daisy Meredith did not eat the bread of tears, albeit no lover had come a-wooing.

The double cabin that Daisy shared with Margot, the devoted Provençal maid, was near the stern. Lady Mary's neighbours on one side were a Colonel and his wife, and on the other side there was a two-berth cabin occupied by a young lady from Calcutta with her maid, a young lady who was too ill or too unhappy to appear in public, and whom Lady Mary had not seen. She had encountered the maid several times in the corridor, a middle-aged woman, sour-visaged and severe.

"I'm afraid your young lady is very ill," she said to the maid one morning. "I heard her sobbing and moaning last night."

The woman pinched her lips, and answered curtly:

"Hysterical."

She brushed past Lady Mary, and disappeared in the cabin.

"What a churlish person to have charge of a sick girl," thought Lady Mary, full of pity for the distressed fellow-creature whose low moaning, broken now and then by a suppressed sob, had kept her awake between two and three o'clock in the morning.

They were in the stifling heat of the Red Sea, and every porthole was open, and sounds were audible from cabin to cabin.

The moaning sound was in the hot heavy air when Lady Mary fell asleep, and she heard it again when she awoke at six o'clock. After that there was only silence in the girl's cabin—and no sound of speech all the morning, though Lady Mary could hear the door opening and shutting, the maid going in and out, the clinking of cup and spoon when the girl was taking her breakfast. No speech.

She thought much of this solitary girl, after her encounter with the cross-grained attendant. Girls are not hysterical for nothing. The moaning and sobbing in the silent night hours could only mean mental distress. What was the sorrow that watched with her in those dreary night hours? Was it grief at being parted from a lover; or mourning for some near and dear one lately lost: father, mother, sister, brother?

And to be solitary in her sorrow, with no one near her but her hard-featured, unmannerly maid! Lady Mary's heart went out to this unknown girl in her loneliness, a heart full of pity and yearning.

"I must do something," she thought. "I can't lie here, night after night, like a log, while that girl hugs her sorrow. Surely sympathy, soothing words from a motherly woman, might bring her some little comfort."

She had said no word about the lonely girl to Daisy, who was all kindness for her fellow-creatures, nor to her maid, Margot, whose exuberant Southern nature would have been quick to pity, eager to console, if it were only by offering to retrim a hat, or devise something new in hair-dressing. Lady Mary felt that those secrets of the night season, the sorrow with which proximity had made her acquainted, were not to be told to the first comer. Something she felt she must do; and one sultry breathless day, when the maid had gone to her dinner, Lady Mary knocked gently at the door of the next cabin.

A fretful voice answered quickly, "Come in," and then, as the fine, matronly figure, the handsome face and silver hair, appeared in the doorway, "I thought it was the stewardess," continued the voice, rather more fretfully. "You've come into the wrong cabin."

The girl was sitting on her sofa-berth—wrapped in a loose white dressing-gown, her hair coiled in a great careless knot on the top of her head, her bare feet in red slippers without heels. Lady Mary's keen vision realised every detail. She looked slovenly, forlorn, uncared for, out of health, but she was exquisitely beautiful. Her face shone in the cramped cabin space, like a light; her form was no less exquisite. The muslin dressing-gown hanging loosely over the lawn night-gown revealed every line of the perfect figure; but, while the matron's eyes gazed at her in startled admiration, the girl snatched up a large soft shawl that had fallen on the floor, and wrapped it hastily round her.

"No, there is no mistake," Lady Mary said gently. "I am in the next cabin; and, knowing that you were quite alone——"

"I am not alone. I have my maid."

"Yes, but she is not a companion for you. Very useful, no doubt, but no companion."

"I don't want company. I prefer being alone—thank you."

There was a pause before the last two words, and the tone was not over-gracious.

"My dear young lady, I have heard you sobbing in the night. I can't help having ears, you know; and I should like so much to be of use to you. I thought perhaps I might help you to think of pleasant things; to put aside your grief, now and then; to take courage, and to face life bravely. No life is all sorrow."

"It is easy to say that. I daresay you have been lucky, and have never known what trouble means. You look like that."

A woman of fifty, as perfectly dressed and *coiffée** as Lady Mary always was, is apt to give that impression; and her appearance certainly made a marked contrast to the girl's slovenly forlornness.

She had drawn her feet up on to the sofa, and sat huddled in the big red shawl, making herself as ungraceful a bundle as she could. But the lovely head and throat, the perfect shoulders, the shining copper bronze of her hair, the large hazel eyes, and red sorrowful mouth could not be hidden. Mary Harling looked at her with a sad reproachfulness.

"I have known a great sorrow, a sorrow that went very near to break my heart," she said gravely.

"I beg your pardon," the girl said quickly, and then, looking at her visitor with great angry eyes, like a wild beast at bay, she said: "And in the days of your great sorrow perhaps you didn't much want to see people—especially strangers."

"That will do," said Lady Mary. "You must kindly pardon my intrusion, which I sincerely regret."

She had left the cabin, and shut the door, before the girl could reply.

"I am an officious old fool," she told herself angrily, as she shut her own cabin door, a little more sharply than usual.

Three minutes afterwards there came an impetuous knock on the panel.

"Come in," said Lady Mary.

The door opened quickly, and the girl appeared, the red shawl skewered round her with a gold safety-pin, and her long white dressing-gown trailing on the floor.

"I am sorry I was rude," she faltered. "You meant to be kind to me."

There was a sullen air even in her apology; but Lady Mary saw the lovely red lips quivering, the eyes strained as if to keep back tears.

"Sit down," she said kindly, and drew the girl on to her sofa, and put a down pillow behind her shoulders. "I did mean to be kind. I wanted to cheer you, if I could. It must be sad to be alone on a voyage, or with only a maid. And yours doesn't seem a pleasant person."

"She's a horror; but I suppose she means well. She is extremely respectable."

She said the last words with a curious sneering emphasis that did not escape Lady Mary.

"She has a daughter who is the very pink of respectability," the girl went on, becoming suddenly voluble. "She is always talking of herself and her daughter. It is her only idea of conversation. Her daughter passed all the standards at a Board School, and went into service at seventeen. She was perfection as a children's maid in a great house; and at nineteen she married the head gardener, and her mistress gave her a wedding present, and she never did anything wrong in her life, never, never, never!"

"That kind of conversation must be rather boring."

"Boring! I turn my face to the wall, and clench my hands, and wish myself dead. I always wish that; but I wish a little more intensely when Wareham is telling me about her daughter."

"My dear girl, you must not say that. We have to make the best of our lot upon earth, come what may. You must let me be your friend, while we are on the ship, no matter how our ways are to be parted afterwards. Have you any nice books with you? Look at my travelling library—my favourite poets—and Charles Lamb, and a Dickens, and a Thackeray or two. At my age old books are old friends. Is there anything there you would like to read?"

The girl's eyes had been roving round the cabin, where there was a gracious elegance in all the trivial conveniences and adornments that gave the keynote to the occupant's life. Down cushions in embroidered muslin covers, with soft silk frills, Indian coverlet and *portière** of exquisite needlework, writing-cases, work-basket, delicately bound books, everything choice and graceful and pretty, the belongings of a woman into whose life nothing sordid or ugly, cheap or pretentious, had ever entered. And Lady Mary herself in her soft silk, middle-aged gown, with an old Mechlin lace fichu, fastened neatly with one large turquoise, was in perfect harmony with her surroundings. Everything had the same air of calm superiority; and everything jarred upon the girl's over-strung nerves.

"I see you have 'Jane Eyre,'" she said, after a pause. "I should like to read that again."

Lady Mary took the volume out of the row of books in the shelf over her berth. It was bound in dark green morocco, with a good deal of gold work, and inlaid with scarlet calf.

"I made her as fine as I could, because I am so fond of her," she said, as she put the book in the girl's hand.

The girl turned the leaves, looking at the pages dreamily, and gave a long heart-broken sigh.

"How happy I was when I read this book," she said presently, "and yet I thought I was miserable. It was at school, and novels were contraband.* That made us fonder of them. One of the house-maids used to get them for us—from the grocer, bright red cloth books, printed on cheap paper. 'Jane Eyre' was the gem."

"Was it a happy school?"

"Oh, pretty well, as schools go, I believe. It was an expensive school. There were only twenty girls, and we had a fine garden—tennis court—croquet ground, and we dined late, and had to wear low frocks for dinner. There was a great deal of fuss; but I think most of the girls liked it. I didn't."

Lady Mary was on the point of asking the whereabouts of the school, but checked herself. She wanted to obtain this girl's confidence, because it seemed to her that the girl had sore need of a friend; and the best way to win her from her sullen reserve was to refrain from asking a single question.

"I'll take care of your lovely book," the girl said, rising to go, and then, as she neared the door, 'Perhaps you don't know even my name," she said. "It is Brown—Jane Brown."

Lady Mary did not try to detain her. She wanted the girl to get accustomed to the idea of a friendly neighbour.

"Pray come in and see me sometimes when you are bored," she said. "I generally stay in my cabin between lunch and tea. Or would you not like to come on deck with me some fine morning? I'm sure the air would be good for you."

"Thanks, no. I hate the deck. And I feel too ill to dress properly. But if I may come here, once in a way, when I want to hear a human voice that is not Wareham's——"

"Pray, come. I shall be very glad to see you. I am generally alone at this time. My young cousin enjoys herself so much all the morning that she wants a long siesta."

"I hear her laughing," said Miss Brown. "She must be a very cheerful person."

"She has a very happy disposition."

Miss Brown knocked at the cabin door at the same hour next day. She was dressed quite neatly in a blue muslin morning-gown, and her hair was tidier—those masses of copper-brown hair, which Lady Mary admired. She brought back "Jane Eyre," wrapped in tissue paper.

"You must read very quickly," said Lady Mary; "but perhaps you have only skimmed the book at a second reading."

"No, I read every word. It took me out of myself. I was Jane Eyre—and not Jane Brown. Her troubles were my troubles. I don't think she had so bad a time after all."

"What, not when she ran away from the man who worshipped her—not when she was starving on the moor?"

"She must have been proud of herself all the time, because she was worshipped by that stern strong man, and because she had fought the battle and won, and had never lost her self-respect. I don't think starving on the moor mattered. She knew he loved her. She knew she had done a great thing in leaving him. I believe she was always happy—always—after she knew that Rochester loved her."

She dashed some tears from her eyes with an angry movement of her hand, a lovely hand, perfectly moulded, only a shade too white for the beauty of youth and health.

Mary Harling was glad to hear her talk. There had been no sobs or moaning heard in the night, and no doubt the girl had read all night, or had read herself to sleep. Anything was better than an incessant brooding on her own sorrows, whatever those might be.

She sat on the cabin sofa nearly an hour watching Lady Mary at work upon one of her poplars, the taper fingers drawing the silken thread in and out, the hand now above, now below the frame. It seemed a work of ages.

"Your trees don't grow as fast as the poplars out of doors," the girl said.

"No, it is slow work. Penelope* might have tired out her suitors without the nightly task of unpicking."

There were lapses of silence, with only the faint rustle of Lady Mary's silken sleeve as her hand moved to and fro.

Presently, after a little speech about indifferent things, Lady Mary ventured a question.

"I hope you are going home to relations you love?"

"I am going to a woman I never saw, though she is my father's sister."

"And you are going to live with her till your people come home?"

"Yes, I suppose so. I have only my father, and he will not leave India for the next three years."

"I hope your aunt is a nice, kind person, and that her surroundings will be all that you like."

"I don't care much for surroundings. She must live in a house with walls and a roof, and there will be air to breathe, and food to eat, and a bed to lie upon."

"I am sorry to hear you talk in that despondent strain," Lady Mary said, very gently. "You are so young, and, forgive me for saying, so lovely, that it is cruel to think you can be without hope."

"It is true all the same, I have nothing to hope for," and then, after a pause: "and everything to dread."

She clasped her hands before her face, struggling with her sobs, then rose quickly, and went to the door.

"I am going back to my cabin," she said, "it always hurts me to talk of myself."

Lady Mary put her arms round her, and kissed her reluctant cheek.

"Then I will never speak of your own affairs again," she said.

"You shall have all my sympathy, without a single question. Forgive me if I stirred the waters of Marah."*

"They need no stirring. They drown my heart day and night."

"Come to me again to-morrow; and we will talk of only pleasant things. And you must choose another book before you go."

"Thank you." The girl surveyed the shelf slowly, then put up her hand and drew out a slim volume half bound in gilded vellum.

"'The Scarlet Letter,'"* exclaimed Lady Mary. "Oh, that is such a painful story!"

"Please let me read it. My father took it away from me a year ago, when I was not half through it, for fear I should learn things a girl ought not to know. Is that your idea of girls? That they ought to know nothing of the sorrow and shame that some women have to suffer. Some who are no older than themselves?"

"It is a difficult problem. I have no daughter, so I have not had to answer the question. Take Hawthorne's book, if you like. It is exquisitely written; but I'm afraid it will make you sad."

Lady Mary woke in the dead of the night, at the sound of stifled sobs in the next cabin.

The "Scarlet Letter" was not an effectual anodyne.

CHAPTER II

THE *Electra* was nearing Brindisi, and a great many passengers were prepared to leave her; cabin trunks, handbags, books, umbrella cases, and frivolities of all kinds were packed and ready for unshipping, maids and valets were busy, and on the alert for the work of landing.

Lady Mary was going home in a leisurely way, meaning to break the journey and loiter at any place she cared for, at Venice, at Verona, on the Italian Lakes, with perhaps a week in Paris, to order gowns and hats, and look about her in a general way. She had friends among the *haute noblesse*,* in solemn houses, in grey dull streets in the old St. Germain faubourg, set back from the traffic of the stony street, beyond the echoes of stony courtyards made more melancholy by funereal evergreens in great green tubs, houses with double flights of marble stairs, and a glass canopy over the door. Lady Mary was a welcome visitor in many such houses, and had the history of their owners engraved upon her capacious brain, with all the relationships, to the furthest cousin, set down as in a funeral letter. She had known the Orleans Princes and their belongings, at Twickenham and Ham, and Bushey Park, and Stowe; and she loved to talk of them. A week in Paris was a treat that she always gave herself after a winter in distant places.

Jane Brown was to stay with the ship to the bitter end.

"I wish you were coming with my cousin and me," said Lady Mary, who had grown fond of the girl, or as fond as Jane Brown would allow her to be.

Jane had come to her cabin every afternoon, staying a shorter or longer time as the spirit moved her. Conversation often flagged, for the girl's reticence made it difficult, and Jane would sit in silence with a joyless face, watching Lady Mary's needle, almost as if it were a penitential task so to watch, a kind of intellectual crank, exercising her mind upon useless labour.

She was always the same, and in those many days of friendly

intercourse Mary Harling felt that she had got no nearer to the suffering soul behind that melancholy outward form. She knew that the soul was steeped in sadness; but she knew nothing of the cause. Her guesses were painful; for such persistent gloom in so young a creature must needs have a bitter root.

The girl had obstinately refused to be introduced to Daisy Meredith.

"She is a good deal older than you, but she would be more in sympathy with you than I can be," Lady Mary urged. "She is still a girl, very young for her age, and so bright and cheerful. She would do you good."

"Please don't ask me, I like to sit here with you for a little while every day. Your kindness has let a ray of light into my life. You—you are such a lady; you are so strong. But I could not talk to a girl. My life will never be like a girl's life again. We should not have a thought in common."

Mary Harling brooded over that strange sentence. "My life will never be like a girl's life again."

From a girl who did not look nineteen such a speech argued utter ruin. Never again. It argued the irrevocable, the mischance that had changed the cup of girlhood from sweet to bitter. A broken vow, a trust betrayed, a young life spoilt.

It was between ten and eleven o'clock, on the night before they came to Brindisi. Lady Mary had dismissed cousin and maid, and was sitting in her dressing-gown, reading one of those devotional books, with which, or with a chapter or two of Holy Writ, she was wont to soothe her spirits before she tried to sleep. To-night she had chosen a sermon of Frederick Robertson's, whose discourses never wearied her, though she knew them almost as well as the Psalms. He was her preacher of preachers, the wisest, the most delicate in apprehension, the most generous in love and pity for his brother man.

There came a light knocking at the cabin door. She knew the hand, for it always seemed as if she could hear it flutter as it knocked, shrinkingly, timidly.

She went quickly to open the door.

"Come in, come in, my dear girl. I had bolted myself in for the

night; but I am very glad to see you. Our last night together! Sit
down and let us have our last talk. The Captain says we can land
directly after breakfast. I shall be at Danielli's to-morrow night. I
wish you were coming with us."

"How happy you look," said the girl, contemplating her with a
kind of fearful wonder, "how serene, and how strong! I mean how
strong in courage and resolution."

"And yet I have had to bear sorrow that might break any woman's
heart. I used to think my heart was broken."

"Was it something very dreadful? The death of someone you
loved?"

"No, thank God, it was not death. But it was only less dreadful
than death. But I don't want to talk of that. You have never told me
your trouble, and I won't tell you mine. Only I want you to know
that though I seem a frivolous over-prosperous woman I have gone
through the valley of the shadow, and the shadow has been round
and about me for six years of my life."

"Ah, but you can hope. You may come back into the sunshine
some day."

After this there was a silence. The girl sat huddled in a corner of
the sofa, her clasped hands resting on her knees. Lady Mary noted
the straining of the small hands, the thin pale fingers interwoven.

"You can keep yourself alive with hope," she said, after a long
pause; and then she burst into tears, suddenly, her forehead bowed
upon the clenched hands, her form shaken by convulsive sobbing.

There came a sharp knock at the cabin door, and the maid's
harsh voice.

"You had better come to bed, miss. It is past eleven, and you
oughtn't to be out of your own cabin."

Lady Mary opened the door and faced the intruder.

"Your young lady is going to stay with me a little longer. I will
see that she goes back to her cabin in good time."

The tone of authority subdued the sour-faced person.

"It is very late for Miss Brown to be out of her cabin," she said
sullenly, and sullenly withdrew.

Mary Harling seated herself by the sobbing girl, and tried to
raise her drooping head.

"Let me comfort you, if I can," she said. "Won't you tell me your trouble? I might advise; I might help you even. I could at least do more than that disagreeable maid of yours. Don't be afraid to confide in me—even if it is something very sad—something that makes you ashamed."

The last few words were whispered, as Lady Mary drew the girl's head to her bosom, and gently smoothed the disordered hair, with a motherly hand, the hand that had caressed her boy's handsome head when he came to her flushed with a day's sport, on the cricket ground, or in the hunting field; a hand that had not forgotten the maternal touch.

"I want to tell you! I must tell you: now that you are leaving the ship, now that we shall never meet again. Will you promise never to repeat what I tell you—never to speak of me to any living creature?"

"Yes, I promise. Nothing you tell me tonight shall ever be repeated by me, without your distinct permission."

"Then I will trust you. I came here because I felt that I must tell you. My heart was bursting. But you will despise me—you will loathe me, when you know."

She struck her hand fiercely on the loose muslin that was folded over her breast.

"The Scarlet Letter," she cried, "the Scarlet Letter ought to be there."

The story was told in that speech.

"My poor, poor, unhappy girl!"

Lady Mary took her in her motherly arms and wept over her, with more emotion than she had felt for anyone not of her own kin. She had suspected some evil thing from the beginning, for the girl's trouble expressed itself in a way that could mean no common trouble. The solitary voyage, the stern-faced attendant, every detail, hinted at a ruined life, a young life destroyed in its bloom, a bud blighted and cankered before it could become a rose. And the desolate creature was so lovely, gifted with beauty that in happy surroundings, in the sunlight of good luck, might have made her one of society's queens. Whatever her fault had been, however deep her fall, Mary Harling's heart bled for her, as she felt the young bosom heaving with convulsive sobs, and the strained grip of the slender hands that clung to her arm.

"We shall never meet again," the girl said, "and I want you to know what an unhappy wretch I am." She went on breathlessly, in short sentences, punctuated by sobs. "I only left school in England a year and a half ago. I went to my father and mother in India. I had not seen my father since I was a child. I hardly remembered him, except that he didn't care much for me, and that he was often angry about trifles. But my mother and I had been parted only two years, and I adored her. I was her only child. There had been another, a son, but he died before he was a year old. We adored each other. There never was such a mother. I flew into her arms when she came to meet me, and I saw death in her face. That was my first sorrow. She only lived four months after I landed, lived and suffered. When she died I was alone in the world, for I knew my father did not care for me. He had another person to think about; someone he had no right to care for. Before the hot weather began he sent me to Cashmere, with one of his nieces, a Colonel's wife, who was gay and bright and kind and easy going, as everybody was in Cashmere. My father went with his friends to Simla."

There was a pause, the girl struggled with her sobs, and Lady Mary waited patiently.

"If you promise never, never, never to repeat what I tell you, I can trust you, can't I?"

"I have never broken a promise."

"After my mother died I used to lie awake half the night longing for her, and thinking that there was no one in the world who loved me. And for the rest of the night I used to dream that she was still alive, and that we were happy. When I woke from that dream—it was almost the same every night—I used to wish that I was dead. But afterwards in Cashmere I knew that there was another kind of love, a love that dazzled me, a love that wrapped me round like fire. I was happy, happy, happier than words can tell."

She clung to Lady Mary, she buried her face upon the matron's ample shoulder, and for the first time that good Christian felt a touch of repulsion.

"I don't know why I loved him; but his influence changed my

life, almost from the day we first met. He was handsome, fearless of man or beast, strongwilled, impetuous. He gave me no peace till he had made me love him. He took possession of my soul, and made himself my master, and it seemed sweet to obey him, to know that he was always thinking about me, and watching, and following me. We were always together. My cousin encouraged him. People said he was rich. He was a great match, she told me, and I was a very lucky girl to have caught him. Vulgar, wasn't it?"

"Hideously vulgar," said Lady Mary.

"Well, we were often together, and alone. My cousin had her own pleasures, and was always busy, so she let me do what I liked. We went for long forest rides. We climbed lonely hills. One evening at sunset, when we had lost our way, he repeated some verses of Byron's—a scene on a Greek Island—Haidee and Juan,* and after that he used to call me Haidee, whenever we were alone. Then one day my cousin made a fuss, and told him people were beginning to say ill-natured things about us; and he must either declare himself, or must go away and never see me again. He said he must go, if she thought fit, for he was not free to marry. He had thought of me only as a romantic child, and had never imagined that any scandal could come of his liking for me. A year ago when he was in America he had engaged himself to a Boston girl, an heiress. Her money was of no consequence to him, for he was an only son, and would be well-off by and by; but he was bound to the young lady at Boston. My cousin told me this, and I listened to her without a word; and she never knew that I was a lost creature, scorched, seared, consumed by the fire of that dreadful love. Think what it was, to have loved as Haidee loved, never to have doubted that I was to be his wife, that I was to belong to him for ever, and then to hear that we must part."

"He was an insufferable villain," said Lady Mary, with clenched teeth.

"Oh, I suppose other men are as cruel, when girls are fools. Oh, the shame of it, the shame," with a sudden rush of scalding tears, "the agony of knowing that I was an outcast for the rest of my life."

"Did you never see him again?"

"Once. He made his way to me at night. He cried over me. He

threw himself upon the ground, and cursed himself, and beat his head upon the floor. He told me that he would have made any sacrifice to have me for his wife, if he had not been bound in honour to another girl, a girl who would die if he jilted her. I think he was sorry—but he said I was so young, and I would forget him, and make a good match, and perhaps be a great lady."

"He did not know——"

"What you know," whispered the girl, with her face hidden. "No, he never knew that. He left Cashmere after that night."

"And you have never written to him?"

"Never."

"But others had to know."

"Wareham told my father. He never spoke like a father to me after that. He arranged for me to go to his sister in Ireland. I am to stay with her till he comes to fetch me. It may be two years, three years, five, six, seven years."

"Poor child, poor child."

Lady Mary found herself wanting in words of consolation. To a woman of mature years, with whom chastity was a habit of the mind, such a fall as this, the fall of a well-born, well-bred girl, was inconceivable. She could better understand the outcast of the streets, the village beauty, betrayed and abandoned, flung into a gulf as black as hell. She was not without pity; but she was without understanding. She wanted to speak words of healing and comfort, but the words would not come. She could only think of the disgracefulness, the shamefulness of the story. A girl, educated at a respectable English school, a girl whose heart was still bleeding from the loss of a good mother, a girl in the freshness of youth, to whom the faintest touch of impurity should be horrible, for such an one to fling herself into the arms of her first lover, consumed by the fire of lawless love! It was unthinkable.

"How old are you?" she asked, almost sternly.

"I shall be eighteen in April."

"Your cousin was as wicked as your seducer: to take no more care of a girl of seventeen."

The girl started to her feet, releasing herself from Lady Mary's surrounding arms.

"You are disgusted with me," she said shortly. "I was a fool to tell you. And some day, if chance should bring us together again, you will point me out to your friends as a disreputable creature, unfit to mix with decent people."

"I have given you my promise."

Lady Mary was of that modern Anglican Church which loves the things that belong to the old Faith. An ivory crucifix hung over her berth. The girl had often looked at it, with dreary eyes, finding no comfort in the thought of a Redeemer. She looked at it now with a sudden purpose, snatched it from the hook where it hung, and put it into Lady Mary's hands.

"Swear," she said, "upon this cross, that you will never give me away."

The slang phrase was repellent at such a moment, and Lady Mary answered stiffly:

"I have promised," she said, "that is enough."

"No, no, no, it is not enough. I hate myself for having babbled to you. I shouldn't have done it if I were not distracted. I must have your oath. I know you are a religious woman, and if you swear upon that crucifix, you will not break your word."

Mary Harling lifted the sacred symbol to her lips.

"I swear never to repeat what you have told me," she said, in a low grave voice, and then, putting her arm round the girl, and making her sit down beside her, she said gently:

"You have been very hardly used—yet you have, I fear, yourself to blame in some part, for the trouble that has come upon your young life—but your Saviour will accept your atonement of shame and sorrow. He has pardoned you, as He pardoned the nameless woman who had sinned, and saved her from the Pharisees' fierce law.* You are very young—and after some quiet years in Ireland, years in which you must cultivate your mind, and try to do all the good that you possibly can to the people about you—the poor people and children that you may find there, and whom you can help and teach—after those years, which you can make years of atonement, you may begin a new life, you may feel yourself a new woman, cleansed and purified by sorrow and good works."

And then Lady Mary repeated a sentence in the sermon she had been reading when Jane Brown came to her door, which had come back to her mind while she sat dumb and unsympathetic.

"'Forget mistakes; organise victory out of mistakes!' That is what the noblest preacher I know of told sinners. But in that happier time which you must hope for, if a good man should give you his love, and ask you to be his wife, don't cheat him. Tell him all your sorrowful past. Don't shirk the shame of it. If he really loves you he will forgive and take you to his heart. Don't palter with the truth. Bear your burden; and be sure that truth is best."

"I shall never marry. I would rather go down to my grave alone than bear the shame of such a confession. I have told you. I could not tell a man: least of all a man I loved. I shall never marry— unless——"

"Unless——"

"Unless I were to meet *him*—free to make me his wife."

She was weeping quietly, subdued, and perhaps a shade more hopeful. Presently she flung her arms round Mary Harling's neck.

"Will you let me kiss you?" she pleaded. "Now that you know what I am."

Lady Mary kissed her warmly.

"Good-bye, my dear. Some day, perhaps, when your life is happier, you will write and tell me. I shall be very glad to know that all is well with you."

"No, no, don't waste a thought upon the wretched girl whose crying broke your night's rest. You have been very kind to me, and I am not ungrateful. Or, sometimes, perhaps, when you open Hawthorne's story, think of me for a moment."

"I shall often think of you; and I want to hear from you, years hence, when you have lived down your sorrow. But, oh, my poor girl," Lady Mary went on, in a lower voice, "if a living child is born to you, don't withhold your love; don't try to put the innocent creature from you. Try, as much as your surroundings will suffer you, to be a good mother."

The girl answered only with a hand-clasp.

"Good-bye," she sobbed, and in the next instant the cabin door was closed, and she had vanished out of Mary Harling's life; or so Mary Harling thought.

CHAPTER III

LADY MARY had made for herself a dignified position in the most respectable section of English society, the people whose country houses were built on land that their ancestors had won from royal fear or favour before the Wars of the Roses, and whose town houses had laid down red cloth for Frederick Prince of Wales, when Newcastle was Premier, serious old houses in sober old streets, where the iron extinguishers that flank the door-step tell of lovely Devonshire's sedan chair and running footmen, of the Gunnings and the Walpoles. Lady Mary's friends were the kind of people who do not worship new money, or apologise for going to the entertainments of Mammon "for the sake of the music," or gobble June peaches while they ridicule the providers of the feast.

Lady Mary's was a quiet world, in which people set a tremendous value upon themselves, exaggerated no doubt, but still a kind of self-respect that kept them out of unclean paths. Lady Mary's friends wanted to know a great deal about everybody who crossed their sacred thresholds, or whose thresholds they crossed. "Who was she?" "What has he done?" "Where do they come from?"

The splendid house, the sumptuous feasting, the costly music counted for nothing.

"No doubt they are very nice; but we don't want to know them."

That was the attitude of Lady Mary's friends to the newly rich, and newly popular.

Writers, politicians, actors, and artists of all kinds were admitted on their merits, and while they were observed to behave themselves properly; but for the bad-mannered man, the bounder or the cad, there was short shrift. Invited once, he was never asked again. Unless he were well-born, and then bad manners were described as eccentricity. The scions of great houses could not do wrong.

Lady Mary had married a great shipbuilder. It was a low marriage, of course, but had been tolerated on the ground of the man's unobtrusive manners, and a certain grave dignity that might have become a duke. His father had been rich before him, and the son had been reared among the salt of the earth, at Eton and Oxford. Lady Mary was a duke's daughter, and had brought her mate ten thousand pounds for *tout potage*,* which was not a liberal portion considering the Duke's wealth. John Harling could afford to brush aside the ducal dower as a negligible quantity, when he dictated his marriage settlement. He gave his wife a thousand a year for pin money, and when a mortal disease came upon him, eleven years after his marriage, he left her fifteen thousand a year during widowhood, to be reduced to five thousand if she married, and to five hundred if she married a man ten years younger than herself. She was only thirty when he made his will, with certain death near at hand, and he wanted to guard her from the evil to come. He told himself that while her boy was young, her plaything and her idol, she would not want to marry; but that later, in her mature years, she might be a mark for the impecunious guardsman or the foreign adventurer.

Lady Mary's portion came from funded property; but her son inherited his father's interest in the great shipbuilding firm, which had been made into a Limited Liability Company. With the accumulations of a long minority, and the increasing prosperity of the business, Conrad would have not less than thirty thousand a year when he came of age; but before his twenty-first birthday Conrad Harling had been condemned to imprisonment for life, and his fortune remained in the custody of his trustees, who were men of position and impeccable honesty.

It was the worst kind of imprisonment, the most hopeless, the most melancholy. Mental specialists, grave gentlemen from Harley Street* and Savile Row, had sat in judgment upon him, and had given their gloomy verdict. For life! They could see no prospect of cure. It was one of those cases of loss of memory which are of all phases of mental derangement the most hopeless. It was not that something had gone mysteriously wrong with the mental machinery, something that might come mysteriously right. The machine was broken. The main spring of intelligence had snapped. The man remained a magnificent man—a picture or a statue of splendid manhood; but the mind was cancelled.

Doctors from Paris, doctors from Berlin and Vienna, agreed with Harley Street and Savile Row.

Conrad Harling—he who had been so much more alive than the ruck of men—was practically dead. He paced the leafy avenues of a park at Roehampton, with a keeper at his side, though there was no need of a keeper, for the house-surgeon's report described the young man as "harmless."

Harmless! He, to be so described, who at twenty had been like Absalom* in his beauty—like Hamlet in his distinction, "the observed of all observers, the glass of fashion and the mould of form."* He who had been a star at Eton and Christchurch, admired, followed, imitated, beloved, an easy first in those accomplishments that youth worships, in one word an Oxford Blue, stroke of the Christchurch eight, captain of the Christchurch eleven.

On the scholastic side he had not done wonders; but everybody knew that he was clever, and at twenty much might be hoped from him.

He was his mother's idol. She lived only to worship him, and to maintain the dignity, the reserve, the aloofness from all unworthy people and paltry things, incumbent upon Conrad's mother. She thought of herself almost as if she had been a Queen Regent, and regulated every act of her life by Conrad's interests. She looked forward to his coming of age as if it were to revolutionise the world, or at least to begin a new chapter in English history. With his means, with his gifts, his splendid presence, his happy self-assurance and spontaneous eloquence, to what heights of statesmanship and parliamentary renown might he not aspire? She smiled when his college tutor told her that he was irregular at lectures, and had very little goût for Aristotle—or Greek tragedy. What did it matter to a Heaven-born orator, who would take the House by storm, and recall the splendid flights of that famous Charles Townshend described by Walpole,* without Townshend's failings?

He would come of age in a year. She had begun to make plans, and to discuss the festivities, the banquets and benefactions, the rural sports and wide-stretching hospitalities, that were to make his twenty-first birthday memorable all over the county. She talked of nothing else to her bailiff and house-steward, in her summer visit to Cranford.

"It is my son's house," she reminded them. "I only occupy it by his courtesy, and when he marries I shall move to the Grange."

The Grange was on the other side of the Park, and its gardens skirted the churchyard. It was Tudor and picturesque, and handsomer than the average dower house; but Lady Mary felt as if she would be laying down crown and sceptre when she left the great Georgian mansion and the family portraits. She was full of brilliant ideas for the coming-of-age festivities—Conrad's birthday was in August, the month of golden grain and scarlet poppies, and orchards brimming over with red and amber fruit, the month of fertility and rich colour, gaudy flowers, and crimson sunsets. Lady Mary would have everything early English, a reminiscence of Frith's picture, "Coming of age in ye olden time."*

Her pet idea was a Maypole dance on the village green, which was lovely and unspoilt by cockney influences. And the Maypole might be left standing, and the young people encouraged to dance on summer evenings. She had reformed the village Inn, which had thriven upon the new system, and was a favourite shelter for cyclists and pedestrians, who were sure of crisp loaves and succulent cheese, well-brewed tea and home-made jam, at the "Harling Arms." Everything in Lady Mary's dominion made for prettiness; and her tenants and tradespeople, and farm-labourers, had prospered exceedingly during her gracious Regency. Nor was there any fear of evil times when the King began his reign. Benevolence and kindness would be the order of the day, sustained by an ever-increasing income from the famous Company in which Conrad was the largest shareholder, with no more arduous duty than to sit as Chairman at a half-yearly meeting, and draw his half-yearly dividends.

And then, perhaps, a few years after that joyous festival, would come marriage, and another ringing of bells and broaching of hogsheads. Lady Mary did not wish her son to marry till he was at least four-and-twenty. She would indeed have chosen twenty-six or twenty-seven as the marrying age, when he had seen the world, and had been in Parliament for two or three years. She wanted him to be free from all domestic cares in the beginning of his political career. Twenty-seven would be best. She knew of half a dozen lovely girls, now in the nursery or school-room, girls born exactly as she would wish her daughter-in-law to be born, in surroundings of unblemished respectability, fortified by blue blood. For Lady Mary's son blue blood was indispensable, although she had descended from her patrician perch in marrying that excellent man, his father.

Having married Mr. Harling she meant that the Harling money should secure a patrician wife for Mr. Harling's son. The girls were growing up for him. He, who was so handsome and attractive, so superlatively gifted in the accomplishments girls admire, cricket, tennis, horsemanship, dancing, would have his choice among half a dozen beauties in their first season. His mother meant to give him a free hand. She would never dictate, she would not even suggest; but she would lead him through gardens of fresh-blown roses, and let his eye and his heart choose the flower that was to be the crown of his young life.

And while she was dreaming of her son's marriage in his twenty-sixth year, Conrad Harling was going mad for love of an innkeeper's daughter, and had turned socialist in his desire to level himself down to her. He was a romantic young man, full of high-flown sentiments and wild Quixotism; and he took up Karl Marx with an enthusiasm he had refused to Aristotle. He gave vent to republican views in red-hot speeches at the Union, reviled rank and state, and raved about the equal rights of men; and he was firmly resolved upon marrying Stella Meadows, whose father kept the "Otter's Head," a favourite resort for boating men.

Within a week of the long vacation, he surprised and disappointed his mother by announcing that he meant to stay at Abingdon and read, and do a good deal of rowing, so as to get himself in good form for next year, when there was every chance of his being in the 'Varsity eight. He would go to her for a day or two now and then, if she was at Cranford, or would meet her in London, if she had any occasion to go there.

Lady Mary was sorry; but after all it was important that he should prepare to face the examiners, and if he could do better by himself in quiet river-side lodgings than touring in Wales or Scotland with a reading party, his mother could have no objection. She did not expect to enjoy much of his society in the "Long." It was happiness enough to see him occasionally, in high health and spirits, to accompany him on a round of inspection on the estate, and to find him pleased with all she had done, intensely interested in the stables and his stud of hunters, in the kennels where his shooting dogs threatened to repeat the tragedy of Actæon* out of exuberant love, in Lady Mary's herd of Jerseys, and even in so tame a thing—from the masculine standpoint—as the gardens that were his mother's pride and joy.

But this year all was changed. He came. He was kind, and interested in her health, and went with her wherever she asked him, stables, farm-yard, kennels, gardens: but it was too clear that all savour had gone out of these familiar things. He would not even have the cloths taken off his horses when they were brought out into the ancient quadrangle.

"That'll do, Brand," he told the stud-groom, "they look in fine condition."

He gave his adoring setters and spaniels hardly three minutes, and left them disappointed, with great brown eyes looking at him reproachfully, as he backed out of the old half-timbered building, where they lived in the broken light from a window in the roof, through which the sunshine came fitfully between the dusk of massive oak rafters.

"Juno looked miserable when you wouldn't notice her," his mother said, as they left the yard.

Conrad was not conscious of the reproach. He hardly noticed anything, except in an automatic way that made his mother unhappy. His mind was not there. His thoughts and interests were miles away. What was amiss? Was it debt? His allowance was on the top scale of college allowances, or a little above the highest scale. But the capacity of undergraduates for getting into debt is supposed to be without limit, and however much they have there is always the something more that they spend.

He had been losing money at cards perhaps; or he had been backing a friend's horses; and he was ashamed to tell her. He looked pale and careworn. Her heart went out to him with infinite pity. If it had been possible for him to squander his fortune in one year of folly, to mortgage every acre, and sell his patrimony to the Jews, and to reduce her to beggary, his mother's power to love and pity would not have been exhausted. She would have gone out of her ruined home with him, hand in hand, as Adam and Eve went out of Eden, disconsolate but not reproachful.

She questioned him gently. She was sure there was something on his mind, something that worried him, and had been worrying him for some time. Would he not trust her? If he had lost money in some rather foolish way he could draw on her for any sum he wanted to make things square, without troubling his trustees. She had a good balance at her bankers.

"You dear old mother," he exclaimed, and he spoke with more animation than he had shown hitherto. "No, I have not outrun the constable; though I did spend more last term than I generally spend—not betting—no, dear. It went upon trifles, foolish things—but no harm."

"But I know you have something serious on your mind, Conrad."

"Oh, a fellow ought to have something to think of besides the college boat. There is nothing wrong, nothing that need trouble you when you are on your knees. But you have hit the mark. I have been thinking of something serious."

"Not the church?"

"What? Turn parson? No, you dear simpleton. That's not in my line. Don't be impatient, mother. There shall be no secrets between you and me. But you must let me take my own time."

He smiled down at her. His face had grown suddenly radiant with the look she loved. She called it his noble look, an expression in which she saw truth and courage and honour, and all good gifts that well-born youth should have. A light flashed into her mind.

Conrad was in love; in love before his time, seven years before the date that her sagacious mind had allotted for his marriage. Some pretty sister of one of his Oxford friends had caught his youthful fancy; perhaps a nobody's pretty sister; a country vicar's daughter, one of many.

But even if it were so it could but be calf-love, a boy's first fancy for a lovely face, or a face that seemed lovely to that ardent young imagination. Such loves are light as children's soap bubbles, look as dazzling in their iridescent glory, and melt and pass like them. She was not going to fret herself if her beloved boy had taken first love, like measles or chicken-pox, a complaint that had to be got through somehow. Her only regret was that the youthful malady seemed to have taken a gloomy form; he was out of spirits, absent-minded, too evidently worried and perplexed.

Even a mother's solicitude under-estimated the evil. For a young man of Conrad's impassioned temperament first love must be disastrous if it be not happy. With him love began at fever point. From the hour he made the acquaintance of the prosperous Inn-keeper's petted daughter, over-dressed, educated up to the high-est all-round smattering point, kept aloof from the bar and its vulgarities, chaperoned by a spinster aunt who never snubbed an eligible undergraduate, but rather contrived those casual introduc-tions that can be brought about so easily on the river, where there is always some kind of excitement and something of a festal air. And one undergraduate having somehow introduced himself to aunt and niece, was able to introduce others, till the heiress of the "Otter's Head" had her following of nice boys, and was established as an acknowledged beauty.

She was very pretty, in the first freshness of girlhood. She had that exquisite purity of colouring, a fairness as of Madonna lilies, from which the idea of virginal innocence seems inseparable. The sensitive complexion, with its quick blushes, the lucid blue of the large wondering eyes, shining through golden lashes, the flaxen hair, all had an angelic character which was so out of harmony with coquetry and slyness that no experience of her cruelty or her want of truth could shake the lad's faith, or startle him from his dream of bliss.

He had known her something less than half a year, and he had been made to suffer every pang which slighted love can feel, every joy that love triumphant can taste. Her smiles and kisses, her frowns and coldness, the moonlit nights when she would stroll with him in dewy lanes amid the subtle scent of hedgerow flowers, and fields of blossoming beans, his arm enfolding her slight form, his eyes drinking the beauty of her face, angelic in the magical moonlight.

"My angel, my wife!" he would murmur in those blissful moments, the heavenly interludes in which he thought she loved him.

Never for one brief flash had his mind harboured a thought dishonouring her. That she could ever be anything less than his wife, the first and most precious of women, was impossible. She was his first and last love. A passion that had mastered heart and mind, a passion that shut out every other thought, and made existence one long dream of the woman he loved, such a passion could have no second.

"It is once and for ever," he said, when she told him that he would go away and forget her.

He had spent the greater part of his college allowance on jewels to deck his divinity; but here that cold common-sense which sometimes chilled him, as out of harmony with the angelic, came into play. She would accept the gifts of her future husband; but she would not wear them as the daughter of the "Otter's Head." People would laugh at pearls and diamonds on an innkeeper's girl, she told him. She was not elated at the idea of marrying him; indeed there were times when she told him their marriage was a foolish dream, that would never be realised. She was a creature of moods and fancies, capricious, unreasonable; and she kept him under the harrow by her cold fits and hot fits, her hours of yielding love, her hours of coldness and restraint.

So determined was he upon having her and only her to share his fortune and rule his life, that, in opposition to her wish, he called upon the landlord of the "Otter's Head" and made a formal offer of his hand.

The man received the flattering proposition gravely, and with something of embarrassment.

"It's a serious thing for a gentleman like you to think of marrying a publican's daughter," he said, "and you're very young, sir, to make up your mind about marriage: hardly of age yet, I take it."

"I shall be twenty-one next year, and I have made up my mind."

"And what about Stella? She's a bit of a flirt, you must know, though I say it as shouldn't. Are you quite sure of her?"

"Yes. She gave me her promise last night. It was not the first time; but it was the first time I felt sure, quite sure that she loves me."

His face was radiant as he remembered those impassioned vows. All her capricious moods, her slights, her coldness were forgotten. She had given him unmistakable tokens of a love fervid as his own. Her arms had been round his neck, her lovely head nestling upon his shoulder, and heart had been beating against heart in passionate unison, while that fond vow was spoken.

"Your wife, dearest, never any man's wife but yours, never, never, never!"

And then had come a flood of tears, and stormy sobs that threatened hysteria; and it had been his tender care to soothe her shaken nerves, to comfort her with happy talk about their future.

And now her father, who might naturally be supposed to receive such an offer with gratification, if not astonishment, discussed the situation with a troubled brow and perplexed manner.

"Of course it's a great chance for my girl," he said, hesitatingly, "everybody knows Mr. Harling. Why, I remember your father, sir, thirty years ago, when *he* was at Christchurch—a famous scholar, I believe."

"Yes, my father took a much better degree than his son is likely to take."

"Never mind that, sir. He never had your form on the river. But to return to my girl. Does your ma know of your intentions?"

"Not yet. She will know in good time; and I have no doubt of her approval, when she sees Stella. She is the kindest of women, and her only wish is for my happiness."

"You see, sir, it don't often happen for a gentleman of your wealth and position—your ma with a handle to her name, I'm told —to marry a girl out of a pub. I'm afraid her ladyship might cut up rough, and make it unpleasant for you."

"I don't want you to trouble yourself about that," Conrad said, with a touch of hauteur. "I mean to marry Stella within a week of my coming of age. That will give time for my mother to know and appreciate my future wife. You see I am not going to work in a hot-headed way; but it was only right that you should be told of your daughter's engagement, and should have no doubt as to the propriety of her conduct when you happen to see her, or to hear of her, in my company."

The Innkeeper was somewhat moved by this speech.

"You're a trump, sir," he said. "I wish there was more like you. And—and you're a great catch for my girl; and I hope she'll prove worthy of her luck—but she's very young, and she's been a bit giddy. You see she's out and away the prettiest girl between Oxford and Abingdon, and the undergrads, and—and—others have made a fool of her. She lost her mother when she was eleven years old, and I've been too busy to look after her much. I sent her to the best school I could hear of—a boarding school for gentlemen's daughters. It was a favour to take her, but the school wasn't doing well, and went bankrupt soon after. She kicked over the traces a bit at school—couldn't stand the rules and regulations. And then I got my maiden sister to come and take care of her; but my sister's a feather-head. She was something of a beauty herself in her time, and was made so much of that she could never bring herself to accept a husband in her own walk of life: and I don't know whether she has been quite the best sort of person to look after Stella."

"Stella has too much self-respect to want looking after," Conrad said.

He knew the aunt, and considered her a foolish person; but he believed in his divinity's intelligence, as he believed in her purity.

"Now, sir, if you really intend to make Stella your wife in a twelvemonth from now, I should like, with all deference, to offer you a bit of advice. Let me send her away from Oxford, and the river, and the class of people that hang about my house. I've kept her out of the business. She never drew a glass of beer in her life; but there it is, you may call a public-house an hotel and furnish your sitting-rooms up to date, but public-house it is all the same. We must get Stella out of it. You'll want her made a lady before you marry her and there's only one way that it can be done, as far as I can see. She was eighteen on her last birthday; so she's not too old for a good finishing-school, a school where they teach deportment and such like. If you'll find out where there is such a school—Leamington, perhaps—or in the neighbourhood of Reading—an out and out good school, where the schoolmistress is a real lady, and can be depended on, I'll send Stella there for a year. I don't mind what it costs. I want to make a lady of her, and to get her away from people I don't like. That's flat!"

He thumped his honest fist upon the table, and spoke with a determination that startled Conrad. It was as if a doctor were proposing some heroic treatment in a desperate case.

"I hate the idea of schoolmistresses. They would make her prim and artificial. They would kill the charm of my wild rose."

"You must have her made a lady, sir. She mustn't stop here."

Conrad argued the point sturdily, but Stella's father was resolute.

"I know what I'm about," he said. "The 'Otter's Head' is no place for her. I've been wanting to get her away for the last six months; and now I'll do it. It'll be the—making of her."

He was going to say the saving of her—but chose the less ominous word.

Conrad had to submit. He told Stella of the plan, in their evening walk. She was angry with her father, and contemptuous about his views. She was angry with her lover for consenting to degrade her.

"I suppose you think I am ignorant, that I pronounce words wrong, and am not fit to mix with genteel people."

He soothed and petted her, told her she was his ideal lady, but she must not talk of people being "genteel." She had better forget that there was such a word in the language. There was nothing derogatory in a finishing school. It was not his idea, but her father's. For his own part he would not have her changed in the most trifling detail. If there were some little differences between her and the girls he had met elsewhere, those slight divergencies only made her more fascinating.

She listened, and was soothed, and appeared to agree to her father's plan.

He left her in hot haste to discover the ideal seminary in which just that last polishing process might be applied to the lovely statue. Just the artistic treatment that would embellish without altering his goddess. He took the first train to London and went about among the few immaculate matrons with whom he was on friendly terms, surprising them by his eagerness for information on a subject that seemed hardly within the range of his interests.

Three out of five knew nothing of schools, and shuddered at the notion of anything but home education for so precious a being as a girl-child. The other two knew hard cases of Anglo-Indian children who had to be brought up at school and each had her pet establishment, her incomparable Misses, who could create the perfection of girlhood out of the most unpromising material.

Two of the incomparable Misses had a handsome house and gardens at Eastbourne, "quite away from the town and the Parade, and all the holiday people, don't you know?"

An abode of refined dulness, Conrad imagined, where a pupil might die of ennui without ever having run against a vulgar person. The back windows commanded a distant view of the grounds of Compton Place. This in itself gave a cachet.

Nobody happened to know of any establishment at Leamington or Reading.

Conrad tore down to Eastbourne by cab and train, catching the afternoon express with a rush, and drove in a fly to Mandeville House, where Miss Mandeville and Miss Amelia Mandeville fostered all that was delectable in girlhood and eliminated every weed in their garden of girls.

It was a sunny afternoon, and the plain white house facing southwest was glorified, every scarlet stripe in the Spanish blinds a flash of intense colour, the lawns and geranium beds dazzling. Nowhere did he remember to have seen such purple clematis, such amber roses, such scarlet cannas. Everything was steeped in sunlight. It was the kind of afternoon that raises an English landscape to the colour-point of Italy.

Girls were playing tennis, their white frocks flashing in the sun— their joy in the game breaking into peals of light laughter. Miss Amelia Mandeville took him round the house and the grounds.

Everywhere he found perfection, the desires and the ways of girls studied with a forethought and sympathy that surprised him. He had supposed that schoolmistresses considered girlhood their natural enemy, and took infinite pains to traverse and stifle girlish instincts. Here infinite pains had been taken to realise every wish, and gratify every natural taste. Beauty was the dominant note. The spinsters had eyes for form and colour, and a catholicity of taste in all things beautiful.

The house stood on high ground, half a mile from the coast, and the sea beheld from afar was a glorified sea, sapphire and gold against the verdant middle distance. Everything pleased Conrad. Surely his dearest girl would be happy there—for the year of their engagement—only one little year before she would be mistress of his home, and all that home implies for a man of large means. Yes, assuredly she would be happy. The change from those unworthy surroundings at the "Otter's Head" would make this place seem paradise.

He remembered that there were details, small differences, in her forms of speech, that wanted refining away. For him all she said was enchanting; but the women among whom his wife would have to live are critical about trifles. They have their shibboleth; and if they talk bad English it must be their own kind of bad English. Upon accent they are to the last degree intolerant; and they would boycot an angel with a cockney twang. And there were accents of Stella's that touched the boundary line of vulgarity, when she was angry or excited. Conrad began to think highly of his future father-in-law's wisdom. Of course it must be *his* privilege to pay the charges of Mandeville House, which were on a scale in accordance with the luxuries and refinements of the establishment.

He rushed back to Oxford by a night train, too late to visit his enchantress. He lay awake thinking of her, picturing her among those happy girls he had seen on the tennis lawn, the fairest where all were fair, the most divine.

He went to the "Otter's Head" in the early morning before breakfast. She was not an early riser, but perhaps she might feel some of his own impatience for their meeting, after his absence of one long day; and she might be curious to hear his account of the ideal seminary that was to make her as perfect in speech and manner as she was exquisite in personal charm.

The Innkeeper met him with a scared white face.

"I've got some bad news for you, sir," he said.

He led the young man into his den behind the bar, the room where he kept his accounts, and where he sat of an evening, with a crony or two, or with his solitary pipe, while his daughter and her aunt were in their drawing-room upstairs, where they could have their own visitors, aloof from vulgarity.

"She's gone. She's gone, sir—cut and run—the—the——"

His speech closed huskily with a hideous epithet that was doubly horrible when linked with the name of his daughter; and then, for the first time since he entered into his fool's paradise, Conrad Harling was told what kind of woman he had loved.

"It didn't seem a father's place to give her away," the Innkeeper said, "but I spoke as plain as I dared. And I thought that having been lucky enough to meet with a gentleman of your metal, willing to make a lady of her, she'd have turned over a new leaf. I never thought she'd have anything more to do with him."

And then Conrad learnt that he had a rival, and such a rival! A prize-fighter, the champion middle-weight, famous in the sporting world, an olive-skinned gladiator, with close-cropped hair of raven blackness, a blue chin, a broken nose, and a drunken wife. He had come to Abingdon for a holiday, while he was out of training, and he had stayed at the "Otter's Head," the centre of an admiring company, an attraction to the jovial bar, a profitable guest.

Conrad had seen him sculling in the sunshine, the muscular arms bare to the shoulder, the supple form shining like pale bronze.

This was the man she loved, the master she obeyed, the brute-force that had subjugated her trivial nature, while the young undergraduate's passion had only flattered her vanity.

She had left her father's house in the early morning, and had gone to Liverpool with her rough lover, on the first stage of their flight to America, where the pugilist had a profitable engagement. The drunken wife was left in an Oxford slum, and Stella's letter, posted on the journey, told her father what she had made of her life.

She was leaving England, perhaps for ever, with the only man she had ever loved. They would be married in America, where he could easily get a divorce, and where he would be a rich man.

Conrad listened in a stony silence. All the life had gone out of his bloodless face. His eyes—those splendid blue eyes—had become dull and expressionless. He stood with Stella's letter in his hand, staring at the words as if they had no meaning.

"Can I see her aunt?" he asked at last. "She knows more than you do, perhaps."

"Yes, curse her. She knows more than enough. She can tell me now that it's too late. They always do, those women. If ever I had a dishonest barman they'd tell me about him fast enough when he was gone. It's a way they have, curse them. They're a bad lot, sir, every one of 'em, rotten to the core."

He threw his cloth cap at his favourite bull terrier, and then mixed a stiff brandy and soda. It was easy to guess where this bereft father would look for consolation.

"Have a drink, sir?"

"No. I'll go and see your sister."

He knew his way to the gaudy little upstairs room, facing the river, the room in which he had spent many an hour with aunt and niece, a favoured visitor. The crochet antimacassars and stuffed trout and pike, the beaded reed blinds and blue ginger-jars, the mixture of early Victorian and cheap Japanese had set his teeth on edge, even in Stella's bewitching company, and he had yearned to see her in the grave old rooms at Cranford, the rooms where things of beauty, curios, porcelain, pictures, hardly counted in the effect of panelled walls and Adam doors and mantelpieces, and all the glory of cedar-shadowed lawns and Italian garden. He found the elder Miss Meadows with swollen eyelids, and every sign of tribulation, but loquacious in her grief. She covered herself with reproaches, and gave him no time to blame her, had he been disposed to do so. Even amidst her incoherence he heard only too much, heard how the sweet simplicity he had adored was the varnish of an unscrupulous coquette, how she had "carried on"—that was the aunt's phrase—with Mr. So-and-So of Balliol, and Lord So-and-So of Brasenose, how the carryings on had begun when

she was sixteen, and how it was only by reason of her aunt's pru-
dential measures that worse things had not happened.

Conrad had to listen while she expatiated upon Stella's artful-
ness and let in strange lights upon the career of a plebeian beauty.
The presents, the treats, the carrying on! Those arms that had clung
round his neck so tenderly, the dimpled cheek that had pressed
against his own, those exquisite lips whose fragrance he had drunk,
were the hackneyed charms of a lowbred wanton.

He heard that cataract of vulgar speech in a strange silence.
He looked as he had looked in the Innkeeper's snuggery, like flesh
turned into stone. Except to ask to see this woman he had hardly
spoken since he came into the house. He made no comment upon
the story she told him. He went out of the house in the same
frozen silence, and walked away with his face to the west, and the
towered city of Oxford saw him no more.

CHAPTER IV

As Conrad had been living in lodgings, and was supposed to have been reading, his disappearance made no stir. The ways of undergraduates in vacation being erratic, Mr. Harling's landlady supposed that her agreeable lodger had gone to his own people on the whim of the moment, and had not considered it necessary to inform her of his movements. The fact of his having taken no luggage was easily explained in the supposition that he had gone home. It was not till after four letters with the Cranford Park address on the envelopes had been followed by a flight of telegrams at three-hour intervals, that the lady of the riverside villa took fright.

She telegraphed to the lady of Cranford Park, whose photograph in an ivory frame stood on the book table in Conrad's deserted sitting-room:

"Mr. Harling left here on Wednesday morning, September 7th."

She followed the telegram with a letter in which she described the suddenness of her lodger's departure, and how, on account of her experience of undergraduate ways, she had attached no importance to the fact.

Then came for Lady Mary Harling a period of harrowing anxiety such as happily is rare in the tragedy of domestic life. Her son had disappeared from the world of living creatures. The river, or the railroad, or the woods and solitary places round Oxford, might hide the tragic close of that young life; but those graves of youth and hope, those last refuges of despair, refused to give up their secret. The most indefatigable search, persevered in without rest or respite for five weary weeks, the investigations of trained investigators, men who had graduated in Scotland Yard and retired upon private practice full of knowledge and experience, could make nothing of the case of Conrad Harling.

The investigators were somewhat handicapped by the instructions of their client, for in the midst of her grief Lady Mary had been so much a woman of the world as to stipulate that the search for her son should be carried on with the utmost secrecy. No detail, no suggestion of the tragedy was to find its way to the newspaper press; and thus the clues that are most often furnished by the outside public were wanting to her private police. Not even her most intimate friends knew that her son was missing. Even the college dons were left in the dark. Her agents opined that *they* could afford no assistance.

Five weeks of agonising suspense, of sleepless nights, or briefest slumbers made horrible by visions of death, and then came a summons to a little seaport town in North Cornwall, where in a humble inn, the resort of sailors and fishermen, a young man had been found whose appearance corresponded with her son's photograph, and whose presence in that locality had given rise to considerable curiosity.

Lady Mary received this summons in Hertford Street, where she had been living throughout these weeks of trouble, in order to be within easy reach of her agents.

The telegram came in time for her to start in the eleven o'clock express for Padstow, accompanied by Daisy Meredith, her only confidant, who insisted on going with her; and in the golden evening sunlight she was sitting in the Inn parlour, alone with her son. He sat by her side; he let her hold his hand; he let her kiss him; but he kept a stony silence, and his eyes looked at her with a vacant stare.

He was quite mad.

His mother was told the story of his coming to that place in rags, with his shoes worn off his feet, and in appearance a tramp, but with a valuable watch, and a handful of gold and silver in his pocket. He had a gaunt and hungry look, and was footsore. A doctor had been called in by the Innkeeper, and had pronounced him mad, but harmless. His madness might be only temporary, a passing cloud. He had been living at the little Inn for a month, wandering about on the hills or lying on the beach all day. The Innkeeper had bought ready-made clothes and other necessaries for him with some of the money found upon him, and had done all that could be done to make him comfortable; but his silence made a barrier between him and the outer world. He sat among the noisy company in the Inn parlour when the room was full of talk and laughter, thick with the smoke of seafaring pipes, sat in a corner by the projecting chimney, not heeding them. He ate the food that was put before him, but showed no preferences, no desires.

The Innkeeper sent a lad to watch him when he roamed about the hills, lest he should try to make away with himself—but he had shown no suicidal impulses. He only wandered aimlessly, or sat staring at the sea. Why he had made his way to that particular spot and why he stayed there who could tell?

His mother asked no questions. She clasped her living son in her arms, the son she had thought of among the dead, and this was much. She took possession of him. The local doctor got her an attendant from Plymouth, and she carried her son to London, and installed him in his own rooms in Hertford Street, never to part with him till the wound in that beautiful mind was healed, and he was again a free man and master of his life. She made up her mind that he should never know the restraints that other mental sufferers know.* She would be his nurse and his keeper. This was Lady Mary's plan, but unhappily it did not work. She had to yield to scientific opinion. He would be better away from her. Whatever chance of recovery there might be, and her advisers did not hide from her that the chance was small, his residence under her roof, the restrictions of his life while he was an unacknowledged lunatic, would lessen that chance. The constant supervision of experienced doctors and nurses was necessary for his welfare. Love could do little for him, love that he did not recognise or understand.

Lady Mary yielded to medical opinion, after a hard struggle. It was true that her love could do nothing for him. He did not notice her coming or going. She sat beside him for hours without winning one glance of recognition.

She had heard the story of his love-madness, from the landlord of the "Otter's Head." She knew that the fever of one brief summer —a lad's extravagant passion for worthless beauty—had withered his young life.

A wanton's perfidy had killed the happy boy whose path lay in the sunshine, for whom she had anticipated a life of fame and gladness. All God's good gifts, nature's lavish bounty, were turned to dust and ashes.

One consideration that influenced Lady Mary was the better chance of keeping her son's secret if he were hidden in a private asylum, lost sight of by the outside world, a unit in the sum of sorrow enclosed by the walls of the spacious wooded grounds surrounding a house on the edge of Putney Heath. So near London that it would be easy for her to visit him, and yet so secluded and aloof from the busy world that no one need discover his retreat. A physician of experience and position was at the head of the establishment, and the system and details were the highest outcome of modern science and modern thought. Nowhere could this martyr of a foolish love-dream be better cared for; and if his reason should some day awaken from the long apathy of melancholy madness, no one need know how the interval in his life had been spent. It would be easy for his mother to tell her friends that he was a traveller in far-away places, in Central Africa, Central Asia, anywhere. Such wanderings are the natural diversions of youth and wealth.

Lady Mary, for whom truthfulness was an instinct, taught herself the delicate art of lying, and in the earlier years of her son's seclusion that new learning came into play, for she was often questioned about him, most of all in the first year.

"Why had he left the 'Varsity?"

"Boys are so erratic," she said, and, having found that phrase, she used it freely to answer for everything.

Her son was all that was good and dear, but he was erratic. Central Africa was his passion. She never knew where he was at any moment of her life. Yes, of course, she admitted, in reply to friendly questions, he wrote to her sometimes; but the postal arrangements of Uganda were not quite perfect. No, she was not unhappy about him. She knew how steady he was, how brave, how clever. Yes, naturally he had companions; he was not a solitary wanderer.

And so this martyr of maternal love spoke of her son while the empty shell, the simulacrum of that which was once her son, was pacing the avenue at Roehampton, or sitting in the sunshine, dead in life, the mere mechanical life of pulses that beat and limbs that can move.

She went to see him two or three times a week, when she was in London, and sat with him in his pretty parlour, where the French windows faced south, and opened on a gracious flower-garden. He never recognised her. He had no occupations, no tastes, no desires. The days came and went and made no change in him.

The summer after Lady Mary's autumn voyage to Ceylon, there came a gleam of hope.

Conrad had taken a fancy to one of the doctor's dogs, a handsome Irish setter. It was the first thing animate or inanimate that his eyes had rested on with interest since he entered that sad world. He patted the dog, and coaxed her to follow him to his room. One day he called her Juno, the name of his favourite at Cranford.

That was the first ray of memory.

The doctor told Lady Mary that he saw in this a faint hope of ultimate cure.

"It looks as if the machine might work again!" he said.

Even this faint hope was much.

The setter became Conrad's constant companion, walked with him, ate with him, slept upon his bed, and his interest in her never diminished. But with his mother he remained cold and unrecognising. Once, indeed, while she was sitting with him, he looked at her, and then pointed to the dog; but he spoke no word. This was the second summer after the winter in Ceylon.

She went to Italy in the autumn, and spent a quiet contemplative winter in the old cities, Perugia, Verona, Bologna, Siena, studying art and architecture with Daisy Meredith, who was always ready to take up any study, to be interested in even any fad, an admirable companion, with a bright mind that caught fire at a spark.

It was while she was at Siena, and before the trunks were packed for home, that there came a letter from Roehampton—a letter that changed the colour of Lady Mary's existence.

"Your son's mental condition has made such marked improvement within the last month that I think I may now venture to give you every hope of his recovery. His brain has awakened from the lethargy that has so long obscured his consciousness of the outer world, and from the hour when he first noticed the house-surgeon's dog there has been a gradual revival of his intelligence, which within the last month has advanced by leaps and bounds. You will be astonished at the change, and, though I would not advise his return to active life for some time to come, I have the strongest faith in his being ultimately able to resume his proper place in society."

Two days after reading this letter Mary Harling was at Roehampton.

It was a lovely afternoon in April, and the beeches and elms, and wide lawns, and beds of tulips, were glorified in the sunshine, and seemed scarcely less beautiful to the mother's eager eyes than the land of blossoming chestnuts and trailing vines through which the *train de luxe* had carried her, speeding homeward, with her thoughts one perpetual thanksgiving to God for her son's deliverance.

She stood at the French window in Conrad's sitting-room and saw him coming towards her across the lawn, alert and active, with rapid step and happy face, handsomer than in his boyhood, his dog leaping about him.

They clasped hands, and he kissed her in the old boyish way.

"My dear mother!"

She could not speak. She was almost fainting; but she was just able to get to a chair and sit down, with her son beside her. The setter made a diversion, by thrusting herself between them, jealous of the stranger.

"You are as fond as ever of Juno?" Lady Mary said, and these were the first words she could find.

"She's a dear thing, but her name isn't Juno, though I call her by the old name now and then. This one is Flirt, Madame Flirt."

The dog's paws were on his shoulders, and his face was being violently licked.

"Is Juno alive still?" he asked presently, and the question told his mother that he knew of the lapse of years.

"Yes, she is flourishing, poor old dear!"

"She must be very old!"

"Thirteen last birthday."

"Yes, I remember. She was five the year I went to Christ Church."

There came a silence. His mother's eyes were clouded with tears as she looked at him, and it was impossible for her to repress all signs of agitation; but he was perfectly calm. His eyes had a thoughtful look, serenely meditative.

Lady Mary looked round the room he had lived in during those weary years. His table was loaded with books, and there was his old Eton desk which she had sent there, hopeless of his ever using it, now open and with sheets of manuscript scattered about it. She looked at the books, Darwin, Wallace, Tyndall, Clodd, and several new books on electricity.*

"You have taken up science!" she said, full of wonder.

"Yes, it is a new world for me. The house doctor here is a dab at electrical science—and we have long jaws together."

"But I hope you indulge yourself with a little light literature, Thackeray, Dickens, and the poets you were so fond of."

"They are by my bedside—my close companions. I have a good deal of leisure for reading, you see, now I have gone back to books."

"And you take plenty of exercise."

"I play lawn tennis or croquet whenever the weather is possible, and court tennis every day. Of course you know we have a tennis court."

"You look in splendid health."

"I believe I am in splendid health. The head boss here says I ought to join you in your autumn trip—India, Ceylon, or wherever your dear old fogies send you, for your asthma. Would you like that, mother, or would you think me a bore?"

This was more than Mary Harling could stand. She burst into tears, that kept her speechless for some minutes.

The house doctor seemed to have been within earshot of her sobs, the windows being all open in the soft spring weather. He came in through the verandah and carried Lady Mary and her son to his own den, where he gave them tea, and where the conversation touched only on the lightest and pleasantest topics, with many inquiries about Lady Mary's winter travels, the pictures she had seen, Juliet's grave, historical Verona, the Cathedral at Siena, the old Palace at Perugia.

CHAPTER V

CONRAD HARLING'S cure was as complete as it had been rapid. He was like a creature new born. His physical powers had been garnered in the house of bondage.

Extreme care had been taken of his health during those years when the mind was frozen. Proper exercise had been insisted upon, slouching habits had been prevented. Every means that modern science could devise to keep the bodily machine in splendid working order had been employed: if this unhappy young man was to have only an automatic existence that life should be the best of its kind. His doctors were profoundly interested in him, as a remarkable case, a man whose mind had been killed by one sudden grief, a passionate young heart which had loved with such fiery ardour that the ruin of his love had been the ruin of his mind.

No one at Roehampton had believed in his chances of recovery, and his cure made him doubly interesting as a case.

The head physician discussed the situation gravely with Lady Mary.

She had kept no particular of her son's foolish passion from him. She had told him all that she had learnt in a long interview with Meadows and his spinster sister.

"He has a very fine brain," the doctor told her, "and all the best qualities of manhood, pluck, resolution, presence of mind, energy, perseverance. I have observed him carefully, since he has been practically a sane man; and I have the highest admiration for his character, a *preux chevalier** as every youngster of good birth and fortune, who has never known the seamy side of life, ought to be. But he has a highly emotional temperament. You'll wonder how I find that out perhaps, seeing what a passionless thing life is in this place. Well, I'll tell you. His dog—that brown setter he's so fond of—was ill. The vet. thought she was going to die. I saw despair in your son's face—yes—a grief that was almost despair."

"My tender-hearted boy!"

45

"You will have to be very careful of him. An unhappy love affair in the morning of life made a wreck of him. You must do all you can to guard against a second shipwreck. He will go back to the world still in the flower of his strength, handsome, attractive, a magnetic young man. He will inevitably fall in love again—and if his love is a happy one his future will be secure. Marriage will be his safest harbour. With a wife he loves he will escape the dangers of imagination and temperament."

"Oh, I hope he will make a happy marriage. I know more than one sweet girl who would be a sweet wife."

And then Lady Mary's brow clouded with anxious thought.

"You do not think it would be wrong for him to marry?" she asked.

"No, no. There is nothing in his case to forbid marriage— nothing in his history. His mental upset was an accident. But we are going to make very sure that his recovery is complete—before he goes back to the world. If you and he are to winter abroad I should advise some quiet place, out of the beaten track, where he may have time to take up the dropped threads of existence, and to accustom himself to contact with strangers, where strangers are few. I have no fear for him. He is a splendid fellow."

"And if—half a year hence—you find his mental health established would it be necessary to tell the secret of those sad years to the girl he might want to marry or to her people?"

The doctor reflected gravely.

"I think you might ignore that history without compunction."

This opinion relieved Lady Mary's mind. She felt she had not lied in vain.

She had all the summer in which to consider her winter abode. Conrad stayed at Roehampton, with an interval of three weeks at a sea-coast village in Devonshire, untrodden by the tourist, where he went with his mother, and the house doctor who had become his particular friend. The doctor wanted a holiday, and he went as the young man's comrade rather than his medical adviser.

Here Mary Harling had the delight of seeing her son in the plenitude of mental and bodily health, rejoicing in his strength, like a young giant, spending long days sailing a ten ton yacht, or tramping over the hills with the doctor, making friends with the fishermen and coastguards, interested in every living creature and in every aspect of nature, as he had been in his early boyhood when all the world was new.

It was the miracle of a mind recreated, a mind that revelled in a world whose beauty had been forgotten in that long slumber of the brain, and where every common spectacle of nature seemed a thing of wonder. The purple of those heather-clad hills, the ineffable glory of those sunsets on the edge of the western sea, the flowers in cottage gardens, the gold hair and blue eyes of peasant children, the rugged beauty of tawny-visaged fishermen, splendid in their rough strength—"the earth and every common sight,"* filled this new mind with joy.

And then there was that other world, the new world of books. Poetry, fiction, history, science, were all taken up with a fierce rapture. Science most of all enchanted him. He threw himself with ardour into the study of scientific progress, of the secrets the universe had yielded up while he sat aloof, as if in Barbarossa's cavern,* and knew not the march of time.

He surprised his mother one day by some casual speech that showed he knew exactly how long he had stayed in the house of bondage. He told her afterwards that he had found her last letter in one of his coats that had been sent from Oxford. The pockets of all his clothes had been emptied, but this letter had slipped under a slit in the lining of a morning coat. When memory revived, the date of this letter, which had been kept in his desk, gave him the date of his captivity.

Seven years. He had been seven years without sense or knowledge.

He was now seven-and-twenty, in appearance younger than his age; for in that long sleep of the mind the lines that thought writes even on young faces had made no mark upon him. He had an almost boyish air and outlook, frank, joyous, alert, eager. He had all the characteristics that make youth enchanting. He would have but to appear in order to conquer, his mother thought, admiring and adoring him. What girl could resist such a lover? Oh, that he might choose wisely, that his manhood might be won by beauty and virtue, after the lad's fatal infatuation for worthless charms!

His mother trembled when she thought of the second ordeal, a passion that might, in spite of all his gifts, prove unfortunate.

The doctors advised that he should not go to Cranford till he had spent some time among unfamiliar surroundings. It was well also, if there were anything in his manner, any slight deviation from common ways, which might hint at the secret of his long seclusion, that there should be time for the strangeness to wear off before he went among his own people.

His mother told him the story she had invented to account for his disappearance.

He laughed, and praised her for her tactfulness.

"Our friends may question you, perhaps," she said.

"About my travels? Let them interrogate to their hearts' content. I will not leave a square mile of Central Africa unexplored. From the Congo to Zanzibar there shall not be an acre that I can't talk about. I will familiarise myself with every squall that ruffles the Tanganyika, with every treacherous current on the Nyanza.* There are books and maps enough to give me every light and shadow over every mile of African travel. I shan't quail before the keenest explorer I may run against. All I want is to know where I am supposed to have been."

This was after he had been at liberty for half a year, and when he and his mother were going back to England, and to Hertford Street.

They had spent the winter and early spring at a delicious villa among hills covered with olive woods, between Spezia and Lerici.

They had been alone together, with only a Christmas visit from the young doctor, Conrad's friend at Roehampton. Daisy Meredith had been given a long holiday with her own people, whom Lady Mary paid handsomely for the entertainment of their daughter, a detail that was scrupulously hidden from Daisy herself, who wondered at a certain deference to her tastes and wishes hitherto unknown in the home-circle.

It was not till the blackthorns were in blossom in Cranford Park that Conrad went back to the house where he was born, the home that he had left, full of buoyant life, seven years before—going back to Oxford in the Trinity Term; and it was in that Trinity Term, in the freshness of the early summer, that his fate had found him.

Swift as the arrows of Phœbus Apollo, a lad's first love had stricken him with its consuming fever. That wild unreasoning love, the first strong impulse of the passionate heart, had exalted a common coquette into a goddess. Dazzled by a faultless face, blind to all that should have warned and repelled him, the impassioned boy gave up heart and mind to his enchantress.

Friendly undergraduates hinted things, and even, after youth's careless fashion, tried to save him; but he had taken fire at the slightest word.

She was peerless, she was perfect. Earth held no girl who could compare with her. What did her surroundings matter? He would take her away from that vulgar world. She was fit to be an Emperor's wife; and it would be sweet humility in her to accept him who had nothing to offer but his money.

Thus and thus had he argued in that romantic dream which had enthralled him—a dream of a brief summer term and a summer vacation, which seemed an eternity of joy and pain, blotting out every memory of the years that had gone before. He thought he had not lived till he met her.

In those placid restful days among the Italian hills, the book of memory had opened itself, and Conrad had spent many an hour wandering alone, and dreaming over the passionate story that had cost him nearly eight years of his life. That was the price of an unreasoning love. Eight years, perhaps the best years, of a young man's life. The miracle was that he had not killed himself in his despairing rage, when he found how worthless a creature he had worshipped. It might be that only madness—the sudden extinction of thought and memory—had saved him from suicide.

He looked back, and went step by step through the old dream, with a calm mind. The love was dead as Babylon or Nineveh—a heap of ashes—a monument of folly, to meditate upon with self-contempt. In the earlier days of his recovery the girl's face came back to him out of the clouds. Her beauty shone like a star. Then little by little, as memory strengthened, he lived again through every detail and circumstance of his love story, and following that story, stage by stage, he saw what an abject fool passion had made of him. He remembered moments of jealous doubt, sudden suspicions lulled to rest by a smile, hard questions answered with a caress. He recalled his aching sense of the chaperon's vulgarity, his torture of jealousy when he saw other admirers favoured, other undergraduates, young and attractive. He remembered the figure of the pugilist, loafing in the Inn garden, or drinking in the bar, or rowing, or playing cricket; a cheap Alcides,* with a certain picturesque beauty of strength and graceful movement; and he remembered that never for one instant had he thought of this man as a possible rival.

The folly, the commonness of it all, sickened him. He did not even want to know what had become of her, the goddess of a single summer. He wanted *not* to know, never to hear her name again; never to see anyone or anything that could remind him of her. Happily there was no question of his going back to Oxford to work for his degree. His trustees had kept his name upon the College books; but his mother would not even speak of the place.

People at Cranford, neighbours, servants, hangers-on, were delighted at his reappearance among them. He was so handsome, and looked so young. Whatever dark suspicions had been harboured by friends or dependents, as the years went by and he was still absent, were made nought by his return. No trace of past suffering shadowed the glory of his manhood. He was the ideal youth, taking pleasure in all the things that youth ought to love.

Daisy beheld him with wonder when she came back to Cranford. She had seen him in Hertford Street, in that agonising interval before his banishment to Roehampton. She had seen him a wreck. She alone was in the secret of his lost years; for even the servants had been taught to believe that his disordered brain was a passing trouble, the natural symptom of a fever, and that he had recovered, and had gone to Africa with a friend. Only Daisy knew the truth; and Daisy's kind heart overflowed with gladness at finding him completely restored. She was glad for his mother's sake.

Indeed, it was impossible not to rejoice in Lady Mary's joy, joy that made her step light as a girl's, her laughter gay as a child's, her hands eager to scatter benefits on the poor and needy.

They spent more than a month at Cranford before going to London for the season; and Lady Mary entertained all her rural neighbours, the people who had been mystified by her son's absence, who had speculated about him, and had lamented over him and pitied his mother, at many a rural tea-table, and who, beholding her young Absalom in his strength and beauty, felt that they had wasted their pity.

"After all, I suppose he was only roaming about the world," said the squire's wife. "Young men now-a-days have such a rage for exploring."

"He had better have stayed at home and taken the hounds," said the Squire. "It would have been more to his credit than globe-trotting."

"But you'll allow that travelling opens the mind," urged a spinster aunt.

"Don't talk nonsense, Juliana. Do you suppose a young man can learn anything from Kaffirs or South Sea Islanders?"

"But the great book of Nature—to see that unfolded!" sighed Juliana.

"Wouldn't he see enough of Nature in a day with the hounds? Do you think there's more education in an African swamp than in a field of turnips, or a forty-acre pasture? I have no patience with the rage for wasting English money on ox-waggons and black porters, while English farmers have to give up breeding hunters, because they can't sell 'em."

The hunting was all over before Conrad and his mother came home; but he rode every day, exploring every bit of country within riding distance of Cranford. He insisted on teaching Daisy to ride, she having come back somewhat pallid and wan from the arid wilderness of North London, and the domestic bickerings.

Why had she not ridden in all these years, with a stud of hunters eating their heads off?

Lady Mary blushed at the question, which struck her as a

reproach. She had thought a governess-cart and a sturdy pony good enough for Daisy, a cart in which to drive herself about among the scattered homesteads and cottages, carrying charitable gifts, or kindly messages, visiting the sick, and making herself beloved by young and old, since she was not of the strong-minded order. Even when she saw things that were amiss her word of reproof in due season was as mild as other people's blessings.

And now Lady Mary felt that a young woman of Daisy's fine health and figure ought to have been allowed to take some more pleasure out of the horses than feeding them with sugar or apples on a morning visit to the stables.

The horses had been there—growing stale and elderly—for eight years, and no one but the corn-dealer and the grooms had profited by their existence.

"I didn't know that she would care about riding!" said Lady Mary. "She was such a thorough cockney before she came to me."

"She would adore it. I asked her yesterday when she was petting Mayflower—the old mare, don't you know, clever as a cat, and quiet as a sheep. She flushed up like a child. You get her a habit, and Mayflower and I will soon teach her to ride."

The habit was procured from a Southampton tailor in less than a week, while Mayflower was being broken to the side-saddle; and Daisy was soon scouring the country by her cousin's side.

"You women have all got light hands," Conrad said. "You've only to learn how to use 'em. And you sit your horse uncommonly well for a beginner."

"And you've a neat figure, and a wild rose complexion that doesn't turn scarlet after a gallop," he continued within himself.

He did not want to flatter the young lady. She was a kind of cousin, and he treated her in a brotherly way that was charming. He carried her off for a ride nearly every morning, forgetting that she was his mother's companion, and ought to be winding silks for the landscape on the embroidery frame, the mill-stream and poplars that Lady Mary had been engaged upon in her cabin when she talked to Jane Brown. He found a second horse for her, and he showed himself so wise in his selection that no harm ever came to her from either mount. He made her play croquet with him, and here she was the adept, and could give him bisques, for which humiliation he revenged himself in the evening at billiards. It was a humdrum kind of existence, but just the existence that was best for him in the opinion of the Roehampton doctors.

Lady Mary began to take alarm. Was he falling in love with Daisy Meredith? Daisy, who was charming as a dependent and *protégée*, but who was utterly inadequate for the proud position of Conrad Harling's wife. Except that she was a good and pure woman, she would be almost as objectionable as the Innkeeper's daughter; for the blood of Lady Mary's ducal race had been filtered through more than one plebeian family before the union of Daisy's parents, and those parents were in themselves particularly objectionable, a husband and wife who quarrelled and parted once a year, who were always impecunious, and always trying some new device for earning money, the man in the city, the woman in the suburbs, singing-mistress, lady-milliner—lady-cook, beauty-doctor. There was no limit to the potentialities of discredit or even of disgrace. Lady Mary would hardly have been surprised to read of Mrs. Meredith's *début* at a music-hall; for the unfortunate woman had a fine contralto voice which Daisy had inherited.

She was surprised to discover the girl so much prettier than she had ever thought her hitherto. Perhaps it was the influence of youth, Conrad's buoyant temper, the rides, the games, the long days in sun and wind, that had given such lucid beauty to the large grey eyes, such a brightness of rose and lily to the fair young face.

Daisy was six-and-twenty, and had talked of herself as *passée*, and had so considered herself for some time; yet every year she saw beauties reigning triumphantly in their seventh or eighth season, growing only of more imperious and world-renowned charms as the years went by, like peaches slowly ripening on a southern wall, where every hour of sunshine deepens the crimson and amber of their bloom.

Lady Mary began to think that Daisy was pretty enough to be dangerous. And then she was the first English girl Conrad had met in his new life. There lay the peril. She was certainly the prettiest girl in that part of the world; but although Daisy as a typical young woman was charming, Daisy's people made her impossible.

Remembering the doctor's grave counsel, Lady Mary told herself that however impossible the girl might be from her point of view, if Conrad set his heart upon marrying her he must not be opposed in his desire. Indeed, his mother must be thankful that his choice had fallen on a virtuous woman. He must not be thwarted; he must not be disappointed. The passionate heart that had suffered so cruel an agony of lad's love must not suffer from the nobler love of manhood.

He must not be opposed; but he might be managed.

Lady Mary announced her intention of going to London directly after the Whitsuntide holidays. "London will be at its best," she said.

Conrad owned frankly that he preferred the country; but he expressed himself pleased to go wherever his mother liked.

"I know you love Mayfair better than the most romantic spot on earth, ma'am," he said, smiling at her.

He always addressed her as "ma'am" in their lighter moods. Mother was a word for confidences and quiet talk, when they were alone.

"I was born there," Lady Mary answered simply.

"That was a solecism. You ought to have been born at one of the ducal seats. A town house wasn't worthy of my stately mother. I think you must have been stately even as a child. You wore your sash with an air, and crushed the nursery footman if he forgot to bring your bread and milk on a salver."

They were settled in Hertford Street early in June, when West End London was certainly at its best, a glorified city, full of people whose only business was pleasure, full of blossoming trees, and brilliant flower-beds, and exquisite frocks and hats, and beautiful faces; full of fashions that caught the eye from their novelty, just queer enough to be called *chic*, and that would be hackneyed and stale at Brixton before the end of the summer.

Lady Mary opened her house as it had never been opened since Mr. Harling's death. Her hospitalities were bounded only by the limits of time and opportunity. She gave two dinners a week, and had people at luncheon every day; but all her little entertainments were part of one deep-laid scheme; to bring the most eligible girls she could find into her son's company, until some day the girl of girls would be found among those eligible ones, and Conrad would marry, to the delight of his heart and the increase of his social distinction. So much in Lady Mary's world depended on a young man's choice of a wife, whether he should double his weight in the social scale or halve it. To marry Daisy would be to halve it.

There were at least ten girls in Lady Mary's visiting book who were eligible; and of these six were beauties, while three were great heiresses, and one was the daughter of a famous politician whose prestige and influence would assure a young man's success in the parliamentary arena.

Lady Mary watched the effect produced by each of these gifted ten; and although she saw her son pleased to find himself sitting next a lovely face, or a vivacious companion, or a girl who could talk politics with ease and discretion, she could perceive no sign of his being seriously impressed.

She returned to the charge day after day, following up a luncheon and the charm of a huge picture hat, with a dinner and the attraction of Parian shoulders and rounded arms. And all this beauty left Conrad cold. He talked, he danced, he even flirted mildly with Lady Mary's eligibles, but he showed no preferences. A pretty girl was a pretty girl and no more. He had no more romantic ideas about them than Peter Bell had about a primrose by the river's brim.* The better they waltzed or the better they could talk the better he liked them; and his mother observed with regret that it was the girls who had done their four or five seasons whose society Conrad most affected. Their vivacity and keen criticism of life amused and interested him.

Everything interested him. It was a mind new born.

The life of the mind was new. Science, literature, art, music, facts, fancies, superstitions, follies, all things were new. At eight-and-twenty years of age he was still in the flower of his youth, strong as a lion; and he had the freshness of a lad of twenty just escaped from a public school.

In the country his horses and dogs had been enough for amusement: in London the novel pleasure of rushing through the air on the last and finest development of the motor science took his fancy, and he had not been in Hertford Street ten days before he had established his garage and become owner of a Panhard and a Mercedes.

He spent his money with a royal magnificence; and, on finding that his mother's income could not afford more than occasional stalls at the opera, he hurried off to Bond Street, and wrote a cheque for a box on the grand tier.

"Now, ma'am, you need have no more trouble about your seats on the Wagner nights," he said. "You will be as much at home at Covent Garden as in your own drawing-room—and I shall drop in every night—when it isn't Wagner."

His love of music was not the educated love. The old operas pleased him best, the operas with stories that he could understand, and melodies that haunted him: *Lucrezia Borgia, Rigoletto, Traviata, Faust,* and his first favourite, *Don Giovanni.*

He had the gaiety of heart which charms. Invitations poured in upon him; manœuvring mothers courted him. He was handsome, he was rich, and of unblemished character, since his mother's intense pride in him was a warranty for his good conduct during those years of travel.

He had not spent too much money; he had not been troublesome; he was quite the most popular young man of his season.

Lady Mary rejoiced in his gladness with a swelling heart, rejoiced with wonder. She had feared that the shadow of those blank years, the memory, however dim, of that long captivity, would never leave him, that through all his after life the thought of what he had been would be a recurring pain, and that he would never be quite as other men of his age.

And now she knew that he was superior to other men: that the long slumber of his faculties had made him a stronger man on his awakening. It did not even pain him to speak of the past, or of things that touched upon the past. He showed his mother a photograph of Stella Meadows in an evening frock, with a liberal display of shoulders and arms. A girl who has no opportunities of wearing evening dress likes to be photographed in it.

Lady Mary owned that the girl was beautiful, absolutely refined in feature and expression. It was difficult to think of her as a rustic Innkeeper's daughter, still more difficult to think of her as the mistress of a pugilist. But at Oxford Lady Mary had heard something about the girl's mother, and a scandal attaching to the girl's birth, which suggested a more aristocratic origin, a patrician lover, a deceived husband.

While she looked at the photograph Lady Mary had a vague memory of another face of the same delicate type, though not actually resembling this face. She tried to remember when and where she had seen it, and worried her brain for half a day in the effort to remember, when suddenly, as she sat in her victoria, stopping by the Park rails to talk to her friends, the scene in her cabin on the *Electra* came back to her, and the face of Jane Brown.

"It is not the face of a pure woman," thought Lady Mary, wondering at this resemblance of character and expression rather than form, the vague something which made one face suggest the other.

Jane Brown had not written, as she had asked her, to say that things had gone well with her. Lady Mary had almost counted on such a letter, as a natural expression of gratitude for kindness experienced in a day of misery. But it might be that things had not gone well. The wretched girl might not have survived her hour of trial, might not have lived to clasp a child to her heart, and to sacrifice, as Mary Harling, who took a severe view of the situation, had hoped she might. In her motherly kindness she had imagined a future of grey peace, perhaps with a husband, some humble-minded Christian, willing to take a penitent to his heart, and cherish her, with a sober affection, as a brand saved from the burning.

But no word had come, and Lady Mary inclined to think that Jane Brown was lying in the last long sleep in some neglected churchyard in a lonely parish, hidden away in the south of Ireland, where the long roll of the Atlantic breakers would lament over the short sin-stained life.

Lady Mary had little time to think of Jane Brown in this joyous midsummer, with her son's animated presence bursting in upon her matronly occupations at all hours of the day. He adored his mother, and was never in the house long without giving her a taste of his company, over and above the social hours of eating and drinking together, those cheerful gatherings in a handsome dining-room which must surely be regretted, as a memory of something that was pleasant, when the chemists of the future have found out a way of sustaining healthy and vigorous life on tabloids.

Conrad's high spirits were a continual feast, and a continual surprise to his mother. From the hour when he heard her manner of accounting for his absence he had treated his African travels as a stupendous joke. That his mother, the severely truthful, could lie for him, was to his mind an astounding instance of maternal love, and to him the African fable was an inexhaustible source of amusement.

So far from shirking any allusion to his travels he led people on to question him; and he was never tired of reciting his adventures in that wonder-world. He had collected every book of travels that had appeared since Livingstone* first kindled the British mind with enthusiasm for African adventure. He had read himself into Africa, and there was no detail of the life—no thrilling moment of discovery, no vivid impression of the picturesque in land or water, mountain or forest, no colour of earth or sky, that he had not absorbed and made part and parcel of his own mind. With Stanley, with Cameron, with Burton, with Trivier,* he had wandered and wondered. He plagiarised freely, but from so wide a variety of writers that he was not afraid of being found out—not even when almost in Cameron's very words he thrilled a luncheon party by his impressions at first sight of the Tanganyika, or when with Stanley he plunged into the blue waters of the Zambesi for his morning bath, and found himself tumbling about among a herd of hippopotami. Adventures with native kings, adventures in dug-out canoes on tempest-tossed lakes, adventures with elephants, lions, antelopes—hair-breadth escapes of every kind—he had them all at the service of his friends, and was admired as the most vivid of colourists, the most graphic of narrators.

His mother and Daisy Meredith heard, and marvelled, and sometimes ventured a grave reproof, which he laughed away.

"The initial lie having been told there can be no harm in expatiating upon it," he said. "And remember, Daisy, all my adventures are true, absolutely and matter-of-factly true, although they didn't happen to me. But I shall have to make them really true some day, for I think I have caught the African fever; and then your conscience will be lightened of a burden, and you and my mother can sleep easy in your beds."

Lady Mary exclaimed and remonstrated. Could she ever know a night's rest if he were a traveller on that Dark Continent where when two go together only one returns?

CHAPTER VI

DAISY's life narrowed to strictly domestic limits in Hertford Street. She had left her habit at Cranford with the hunters and shooting dogs, the mallets and billiard balls, all things belonging to the life that she and Conrad had led together, in frankest friendship, almost as brother and sister. He had brought a couple of hacks to London, and he rode in the Row before breakfast; but Lady Mary had set her face rigidly against Park riding for Daisy Meredith.

"I let you have your own way about her in Hampshire," she told her son, "but I don't want you to go on spoiling her now we are in London, where I really can't do without her."

Conrad gave way without a struggle; and his mother assured herself that he was not in love. A lover would not have been so reasonable. He told Daisy that she should ride to hounds in October; and whenever there were ladies on his motor she was one of the party.

There was no desertion of his rural comrade. Conrad was always kind after his fraternal fashion; but he was tremendously in request, and had very little time to spare. He went to dances that Daisy did not hear of, choice balls in great houses, where from five-and-twenty to fifty of the *fine fleur* of young manhood were entertained at a sumptuous dinner in order that they might condescend to dance.

Daisy thought herself lucky if she went to three balls in a season, chaperoned by one of Lady Mary's good-natured friends. She used to awake in the warm summer night, hearing carriage wheels rolling up and down the narrow street, and picturing to herself the brilliant scene in Park Lane, or Stanhope Street, or Berkeley Square, or Grosvenor, or Belgravia, and picturing Conrad Harling as the grandest, handsomest, most utterly delightful young man there.

It was after one of the biggest balls of the year, when the

summer and the season were at the zenith, that Conrad expressed himself more enthusiastically than usual. It was the finest ball he had ever seen.

"I suppose the flowers were something wonderful," suggested Daisy.

"Fairy-land. A week's food for an East End parish squandered on lilies and roses. Walls of roses, pyramids of lilies; words cannot paint the splendour."

"And the supper?" inquired Lady Mary.

"*Gunter cum Gargantua*, an endless web of peaches and asparagus and ortolans* and quails, young turkeys stuffed with truffles, hams stewed in champagne, everything expensive that a greedy man could imagine. I took a turn in the Green Park when I came away, and saw the tramps lying asleep in the pale green light, with open mouths, and faces the colour of death."

Lady Mary sighed, and Daisy sighed. To them as to Conrad the contrast was dreadful. Everybody feels the same sharp pang, and forgets all about it three minutes afterwards.

"And the people?" inquired Daisy. "Were all the pretty people there?"

"All, married and single—and one over."

"Who was that?"

"The new beauty. It seems I ought to have heard of her, though she only came to London a week ago, after all the drawing-rooms were over. She was supposed to have been presented in Dublin last winter, a Dowager told me. As if it mattered when, where, ever, or never? She looks as if she had dropped from a star, too ethereal for earth."

"Did you dance with her?" Daisy asked, with a throb of heart-pain.

"Two waltzes. She waltzes divinely. I felt like a cyclops embracing a sylph."

"You haven't told us who she is," said Lady Mary, with whom the who was more essential than the what.

"Oh, she is quite quite, don't you know; an only daughter with a young step-mother. Her father is Sir Michael Thelliston, the General who distinguished himself by his management of that little

Gold Coast scrimmage the other day—or, at least, made people believe it of him."

"Is she an only daughter?"

"An only child. The step-mother is a gushing person, and told me all about her husband, and all about Irene. That's her name, and she looks it. I want you to call upon Lady Thelliston, ma'am, at your earliest convenience. This afternoon, if you like."

Lady Mary smiled at him across the cosy round table. They breakfasted in the library, a room with an old-fashioned bow-window opening into a morsel of garden, which was full of flowers that were brought there in their beauty and taken away directly they had done blooming, like young beauties in a Sultan's seraglio.

Lady Mary smiled, and told herself that the spark had been found, the young heart had taken fire. This new beauty had only to appear and to conquer, where her garden of girls had been impotent to charm.

"Is Miss Thelliston much prettier than all the other pretty girls you know?" she asked.

"Prettier? Oh, I don't know how to measure prettiness. She is almost too exquisite to be mortal—like those marvellous orchids that seem too beautiful to be only flowers."

"You talk as Romeo talked of Juliet."

"Do I? What would I not have given for Juliet's balcony last night—to have had a long jaw with her after the ball?"

"Well, I'll call upon Lady Thelliston—since I suppose they are new-comers."

"Quite new; mere babes in the wood from a society point of view. He has been fighting all his life—in India—Egypt—Africa—always doing well—according to the wife—but never coming to the front as he did in the West African row.* Call this afternoon, ma'am, if you please. I should like to know what you think of the step-mother."

"Do you know where they live?"

"Yes, in a slip of a house in Chapel Street—with a front that looks like a ladder of flower-boxes."

"How did you come to know the house?"

"She rides every morning—in point of fact, I rode with her this

morning—I walked my horse that way—and saw her mount. She
has an Arab that her father brought from India for his wife—who
had been married before, by the way, to another soldier—and the
wife doesn't like the horse—in point of fact, can't ride. And so her
step-daughter has the reversion of him."

"And she told you all this in two waltzes," exclaimed Daisy.

"The step-mother told me. Miss Thelliston is not loquacious."

"Does the young lady ride alone?"

"No; her father rides with her, but he was under the weather
this morning, and she had only her groom. She was dancing at
three o'clock, and in the Row before eight. She is not one of your
rest-cure girls* who lie in bed reading French novels till it's time to
dress for lunch."

"I hope there are no such girls," said Lady Mary, with whom
getting up early was a part of religion.

Conrad could scarcely be more eager about his mother's visit to
Lady Thelliston than she herself was to become acquainted with
the girl who had attracted her son. The history of Conrad's future
life must needs be coloured by the woman he loved and married.
That he should choose wisely, now in the flower of manhood, he
who had so unwisely chosen in his early youth, was of infinite
importance. She had been told that he must not be thwarted in
a second love-affair, that to keep the balance of that fine mind,
now perfectly adjusted, there must be no new love-trouble. He
had loved with an intensity of passion rare in early youth, a con-
centration of purpose that indicated unusual strength of will and
unusual sensitiveness. To cross his will now, to come between him
and the desire of his heart, might be fatal. His doctors had signified
as much; and his mother thought of this sudden fancy with a thrill
of fear.

He had talked of the new beauty with boyish lightness, too
openly, perhaps, for real feeling; but a fancy begun so lightly might
grow into passion; and, oh, what a lifetime of joy or sorrow might
have begun among the roses and lilies of last night's ball! Romeo's
tragedy of swift sudden love began at such a festival, among the
lights and music in the joyous crowd.

Mary Harling felt that her peaceful days were over. She was on the threshold of a passionate drama, the drama of her son's destiny.

Was the girl a lady? That is the first question a woman of Lady Mary's *milieu* asks. Sir Michael Thelliston's daughter was at least of decent birth, and must have been decently brought up; but Lady Mary had met with girls of superior lineage and expensive education who were *not* ladies. Those were, of course, the exceptions that prove the rule; but what if this girl were an abnormal specimen, and not a lady? Conrad had declared that she was "quite quite," and after all that he had suffered for the sad mistake of his boyhood he was surely, of all men, the least likely to be captivated by the loveliest girl in London, if she were bad style.

Bad style was Lady Mary's *bête noire*. She went about the world with a suspicious eye, finding it in unexpected places. That girl on the steamer, for instance, with the hideous phrase: "Don't give me away," in the midst of her tragedy. She had never forgotten her shudder of disgust even in a moment of pity. That girl was undoubtedly bad style; and all that had happened to her in Cashmere had been more or less the result of bad style; a chaperon with neither morals nor manners, a lover who was not a gentleman; the kind of life Lady Mary had read about in Anglo-Indian stories.

Slang was interwoven with Conrad's speech, but slang had to be forgiven in a man, like smoking, and sporting papers, and motors, and bull-dogs; but a slangy phrase from woman's lips was intolerable.

Lady Mary went alone to pay her visit. She often took Daisy with her on such pioneering calls, when she had been asked to be civil to some friend of her friends; but this was too solemn an occasion. She wanted to be alone, to have all her senses about her. She wanted to weigh the girl and the step-mother in her judicial balance, which she could hardly do if Daisy and the girl were keeping up a trivial chatter at her elbow.

She went early in the afternoon, wishing to be the only visitor.

She looked up disapprovingly at the tall narrow house, the ladder of flower-boxes, scenting bad style in that flamboyant façade. There were too many flowers, and the effect was garish. Yet Lady Mary liked colour, and would have admired the joyous dazzle of trope-lium and lobelia, pink geranium and sulphur marguerites, on any other façade. She went into the house with a sinking heart. It had come too soon, the manhood's love which she feared, the love that must be satisfied.

In the narrow entrance hall, and on the narrower staircase, everything was gay and pretty: the white woodwork, the white wallpaper, over which gigantic pink roses clustered and clambered, the moss-green velvet pile that covered every inch of the stairs and landing. In the drawing-room where the visitor found herself alone, there was the same gay colour. It was the house of a *petite maîtresse*, a house like a *bonbonnière*,* and it seemed almost too diminutive to be a real house after the spaciousness of the old family mansion in Hertford Street, where all Lady Mary's audacities in the way of colour had failed to give an air of gaiety. This box of a house on the sunny side of the street sparkled and glowed like a bed of summer roses.

The step-mother appeared before the visitor's eager eyes had time to disentangle the elements of prettiness, china, water-colours, miniatures, bonbon-boxes, hot-house flowers, scent-bottles, fans.

"How more than sweet of you to come so soon," Lady Thel-liston exclaimed, with outstretched welcoming hand. "Mr. Harling told us he would ask you to call—but we thought even if you were so good as to come, it might be ages first."

"I like to know all my son's friends," Lady Mary said, in a quiet voice. "He—he so much enjoyed his dance with Miss Thelliston. He says she waltzes divinely."

Even in saying these few words she had time to discover that the step-mother had been remarkably handsome, and that her complexion came out of bottles. As a work of art she was faultless: her hair, figure, hands, eyebrows; but Mary Harling shivered at the thought of her as Conrad's mother-in-law.

"Isn't she wonderful? Buried alive in an out-of-the-way corner of the South of Ireland ever since she began to grow up, and yet the most delicious dancer, and more accomplished in every way than one girl in a hundred."

"Is Sir Michael Thelliston an Irishman?"

"Intensely Irish, though I'm happy to say a long life in India has only left him a suspicion of their dreadful accent."

"And Miss Thelliston was educated at home—in her father's house?" questioned Lady Mary, wanting to find out everything about these people, but painfully reminded of previous visits in strange drawing-rooms to inquire about the character of an upper servant.

"My poor Michael has no Irish home; he sold every acre ages ago, when he saw things were going from bad to worse. Our sweet Irene has been vegetating under the care of a spinster aunt—Roman Catholic—and a bigot at that."

Lady Mary was dumb. She had been seized with an inward trembling, which made her look forlornly at the nearest gold and crystal scent bottle, wondering whether it held eau-de-cologne, or any other reviving essence.

"It was not her father's fault that she was not having a good time in India. The climate was her only enemy. He sent her to Cashmere, but even that divine climate didn't suit her—so there was nothing to be done but send her home. It was before our marriage, and the poor man had no one to advise or help him. And then came the West Coast war, and his regiment left India, a month after our wedding day. Hard lines for me, wasn't it?"

Lady Mary murmured something, with dry lips; and Lady Thelliston, always charmed to talk of herself, went on blandly:

"But it was all for the best—and the little African war did more for Michael than Burma* or Waziristan,* and he got his K.C.B.* just in time, after a long, hard-working career, and very few chances. I came home to find a house, and furnish it, and get everything ready for my dear old man; and the first thing I made him do for me when he came from Africa was to take me to Ireland to see my new daughter."

Again a murmur from dry lips, a despairing look in a face that seemed frozen. Lady Thelliston, admiring her own coiffure in a narrow panel of looking-glass, meandered on complacently:

"What a revelation! I expected a clumsy, over-grown, potato-fed girl, with a thick brogue, and no manners; and I found a gem of the first water: a girl pretty enough to make what people call 'the match of the season.' I thought of Tom Moore's lovely song, 'Full many a gem of purest ray,'* don't you know, and I insisted on bringing her to London with us. She has only been here three weeks, and she can hardly walk in the Park in peace. People stare atrociously, and I saw women standing on chairs to look at her last Sunday—the women who come on chars-à-bancs* from Brixton. *Enfin*, my step-daughter is talked about everywhere as the new beauty."

"Is she pleased with her success?" Lady Mary asked, finding a voice at last, a voice that sounded not her own.

"If she is she doesn't show it. She's rather a curious girl. If she were not so lovely I should call her strong-minded," added Lady Thelliston, as if the union of mind and beauty were impossible.

The door was opened quietly, and the new beauty appeared, tall and slender, with loosely-coiled hair that held the sunlight, and dark eyes that were like deep waters.

She was the girl Mary Harling expected to see, but glorified. The troubled countenance, the sullenness of despair, the slovenly garments, had obscured much of that delicate beauty, and there had been the indefinable suggestion of a lost woman that had shocked and pained even a heart inclined to pity.

To-day she looked as pure as a June lily, her simple white frock perfection, her coiffure admirable, her pose graceful and dignified.

"Mr. Harling did not forget his promise," said the step-mother, smiling at her. "Lady Mary, this is my daughter, Irene, who greatly enjoyed her dances with Mr. Harling."

"It is so seldom one's partners are as good as Mr. Harling," the girl said quietly, while Lady Mary looked at her in silence.

The girl's calm outlook, and steady accents, took her breath away. That she could stand before her there, smiling, unabashed, with the air of a young Princess accustomed to adulation, disgusted the woman who had been kind to her in her day of shame. She did not consider that there had been time for Irene Thelliston to prepare her mind for this encounter, to muster all that she had of courage, or of audacity, to face the situation. Nor did she reckon with the defiant attitude of a girl who had lately discovered that she was eminently beautiful, and had the world at her feet.

"What an actress," thought Lady Mary, and she was thankful for the loquacity of the step-mother, who expatiated upon last night's ball: the pretty people who were there, the harridans and horrors who ought not to have been there, the ortolans and peaches, the scraggy shoulders and painted faces, the band, the rose-wreathed staircase and the royal guests.

She gave a cover to Lady Mary's silence and enabled her to make her escape, with a somewhat hasty adieu.

While Lady Thelliston rang the bell, the girl followed the visitor to the landing, as if by an instinct of politeness; but directly they were outside the mask dropped, and something of the old trouble came into the dark eyes, and trembled on the lips.

But the girl spoke no word. She only looked at Lady Mary very earnestly, and made the sign of the cross, an instant before the butler appeared to conduct the guest to the door, where the unexceptionable footman and the unexceptionable Victoria waited. The visit had not lasted a quarter of an hour, but Mary Harling went out into the sunshine dazed, her mind paralysed.

"Home," she told the servant, as she sank into her seat, and footman and coachman wondered.

Home was all she wanted. She was not equal even to driving round the Park. She wanted to shut herself in her own room; her bedroom, where nobody but her maid would come; and to think out the situation.

"He must not marry her, he must not marry her."

The words repeated themselves in her brain, like the strokes of a hammer. And then came that other thought. He must not be thwarted.

There was the horror of it.

And then there was her oath, the only vow that she had ever made upon that sacred symbol. In her well-ordered life there had been no need of oaths, no secrets to keep, until her son's breakdown obliged silence. She remembered how the girl had pushed the crucifix into her reluctant hand, and how her lips had rested on the sacred form. Could that distracted girl, bowed to the dust by her disgrace, ashamed, and angry with the fate that had put shame upon her, could that crouching figure, those eyes hiding from the light, be one and the same as the dazzling vision of to-day, so pure looking and ethereal?

The oath bound her. She could give her son no word of warning, for what manner of warning would serve if it were less than a revelation of the girl's history? What other obstacle could be put in the way of ardent love? Unless she could tell him that the girl he admired was a fallen creature she could not hope to influence him. She could only hope what most people hope in the face of a threatened misfortune, that the danger would blow over. This sudden fervour, this impetuous fancy for a lovely face, might pass and leave no permanent impression. Was it not

> "too rash, too unadvised, too sudden,
> Too like the lightning, which doth cease to be
> Ere one can say it lightens?"*

She tried to believe that her son's ardour indicated a caprice and not a passion. But if it were otherwise—if he were to fall seriously in love with Irene Thelliston, well—she had weapons, even if tied on one hand by her oath, and on the other by her dread of opposing her son's will. She would fight for her beloved. It should be war to the death between her and this audacious girl, who could presume to greet her with a placid smile, pure and innocent-looking as Mary when she listened to the Divine Messenger.

She wondered if in every crowded ball-room, in every throng of girlish faces, there were secrets as foul as this.

"I must fight for my son," she said to herself, and then began to meditate upon the weapons she could use.

Could she carry him to the other end of the world with her, pretend an ardent desire to visit the Antipodes, and persuade him to take her there? He was so kind, so indulgent to all her wishes, that if he were fancy-free it would be the easiest thing to make him forego all the pleasures of an English winter, the hunting and shooting that his soul longed for, and take upon himself the toil and burden of a journey round the world, to do her pleasure. But if he were no longer fancy-free, if his heart were touched, to propose such an exile would be to ensure a refusal. He would see through the manœuvre, and resent the attempt to part him from his enchantress.

No! It was to the enchantress herself she must appeal: even if she had to sue *in formâ pauperis*,* urging the inferiority of such a marriage for the new beauty. The girl who was expected to make the great match of the season could very well afford to refuse a commoner with thirty thousand a year.

She would appeal to Miss Thelliston's vanity, to her ambition, to her greed of wealth; or remembering her impressions on board the *Electra*, and believing that there was some good in the creature whose remorse for sin had been so keen an agony, she would take a higher ground as a mother pleading for her son. She would appeal to the girl's better feelings.

"You have all the world before you to choose," she might say. "Let this man go. What can it matter to you?"

CHAPTER VII

HAVING resolved upon the thing that she must do Lady Mary was able to compose her spirits, and to appear in the drawing-room at a quarter-past eight, with the usual placid and reposeful air. She dined at half-past eight in summer, so as to allow Conrad one more half-hour of sunshine and open air—or perhaps a rubber in the card-room at Arthur's. Daisy was always dressed early, and she liked to amuse herself at the piano till Lady Mary came down. It was her idle half-hour after the last letter had been written, Daisy's chief duties lying in the epistolary line.

There was daylight still at half-past eight, and only the reading-lamps on the tables had been lighted, amber-shaded lamps that made for prettiness in the large, lofty rooms with their gilded Louis Seize furniture, and turquoise blue hangings. There were some fine pictures of the decorative order, a Leighton, a Poynter, a Frank Dicksee, two classical subjects by Albert Moore, a dog and a girl by Briton Rivière, and an Alma Tadema that sparkled like a gem:* pictures chosen years before, when Mr. Harling refurnished his father's house for his young wife. The rooms had a large splendour utterly unlike the *petite maîtresse* air that Lady Mary had objected to in the Chapel Street drawing-room. There were books on all the tables, and there was Lady Mary's embroidery frame under a silken cover—but the costly frivolities that crowd modern tables and make them useless as tables were not there. The only ornaments were a few pieces of Sèvres in a pair of old French buhl and ormolu cabinets.

If punctuality is the politeness of Princes it is also the homage of sons, and Conrad's usual way was to be in the drawing-room at least ten minutes before dinner was announced. It was the moment in which he told his mother the news of the day: who was alive and who was dead among illustrious invalids; who was in and who was out in the bye-election; what horse had won, or which side was beaten at Lord's. Although these latter results neither troubled nor excited her, she liked to hear of them from him, and would even affect an interest in racing and cricket.

This evening he only appeared two minutes before the butler, bright-eyed and flushed, fastening the last button of his waistcoat as he came into the room.

"Why weren't you in the Park this evening, ma'am?" he asked gaily. "I looked for your Victoria in the usual spot, and ever so many people asked me why you weren't there. The finest afternoon this summer!"

"I thought you were going to Windsor on your motor, as you arranged with Captain Selkirk on Wednesday."

"I let Selkirk go alone, with his wife. They were only married in February, and they would rather have a long *tête-à-tête* than my company."

"And were you all the afternoon in the Park?" Daisy asked.

"I was there in the golden hour when the river of life is at the flood—when the Bobbies are clearing the road for the Queen, and when there's not a chair to be had for love or money."

He gave her his arm, and they went downstairs, Lady Mary following in a stately solitude. Even in that one flight of stairs she had time to ask herself why she had ever been so demented as to object to Daisy as a wife for her son, why she had not encouraged his liking for the poor cousin, and done all in her power to keep him in the country, where Daisy was a bright particular star among the rather plain daughters of the Squires and Squireens, and of the one great nobleman, whose four over-grown girls nobody had been induced to bid for.

How well adapted they were for each other; Daisy just tall enough for good style, her neat shining head a little above Conrad's shoulder, not insolently over-topping him.

Everything about Daisy was satisfactory, her manners, her clothes, the songs she sang, her way of thinking—everything. Indeed, it was only natural that Lady Mary should approve of a girl who was the work of her own hands. All the refinements of Daisy's education, all the things that had formed her taste and improved her mind—travel, books, nice people—had come to her from Lady Mary. She had gone to Hertford Street a raw girl—with one shabby box, and a flavour of Bohemia in her manner, and she was now, in Mary Harling's opinion, a perfect specimen of gentle blood and gentle rearing. She was good style. Lady Mary had done for her what Nature did for Wordsworth's Lucy.* She had made her a lady of her own.

And Conrad had been in a fair way to love this girl; he had been perhaps on the threshold of a *grande passion* for Daisy Meredith, when his mother nipped the delicate flower in the bud, and brought him to London, to fall into the toils of Jane Brown.

There was less talk than usual at dinner. Daisy was thoughtful even to sadness. Conrad played the agreeable rattle while the fish was being eaten, and fell into preoccupied silence during the rest of the meal; but not till he had questioned his mother anxiously about her health.

"I can't understand your staying at home in such delicious weather, ma'am, unless you were feeling not quite up to the mark—a chill—a headache—or something."

"No, I was quite well. But one may tire even of the Park."

"It's rather like a superior kind of treadmill—compared with a rush on a motor," said Daisy.

"Never mind, Daisy, you shall have a motor rush before long. We'll make up a cosy little party and go to Henley to tea. The Selkirks, and you, and perhaps Sir Michael and Miss Thelliston. And my mother might run down by rail and meet us. Wouldn't that be rather jolly?"

Daisy in a voice of inexpressible sadness replied that it would be too delightful for words.

The butler handed wines, of which one glass was taken by Conrad, and fruit, which nobody would look at.

"I thought they'd never go!" said Conrad when the second pair of black silk stockings had vanished behind the noiselessly closed door, then turning to his mother eagerly: "Well, you saw them both, ma'am. You went early, like a brick, and found them at home. Come now, what do you think of them? How about first impressions?"

His manner was gay, but Daisy could see that he was nervous, apprehensive of he knew not what, eager, impatient.

"I think Lady Thelliston is a very meretricious person."

"Patronises the beauty-doctors, supplements nature with art? Well, she must have been remarkably handsome *dans le temps*,* so there's some excuse."

"There is no excuse for a lady rouging her cheeks like a person in the Burlington Arcade."*

This for Lady Mary was equivalent to a torrent of bad language from another woman.

Conrad looked surprised, and then laughed.

"Oh, my dear mother, how old-fashioned you are! Rouging her cheeks! As if modern art stopped at such primitive measures. Do you think when middle-age comes upon an attractive woman she has only to buy herself a pot of rouge and a hare's-foot.* She must have beauty-specialists, massage, electricity, and give her complexion at least two hours a day of serious toil. It's a mercy if she doesn't resort to surgery and have her face flayed and get herself a new complexion. At least that's what my partners tell me about their aunts. But let us pass Lady Thelliston, and tell me what you think of her step-daughter."

"I saw her only for a few minutes. She is very handsome, I have no doubt."

"You speak with such an uncertain tone. But your own eyes beheld her. You must have seen that she is lovely. Did you ask them to lunch, or to dinner? They go out a great deal: but I hope they could give you a day."

"A verbal invitation, in a ten-minutes' call! My dear Conrad, that's hardly my way of inviting people."

"You do not seem to have been very effusive."

"I did what you wished me to do."

"You called upon them—like the Vicar's wife on a new parishioner. But I want you to make them your friends—to bring them here. I want Daisy to be kind to Irene, who is a stranger in London."

"She won't be long a stranger, if everybody is raving about her like you," said Daisy.

"When can you ask them to dinner, mother? Get them to name an early date. It can fit in with one of your innumerable dinners. The season is half over, so there is no time to lose."

"Have you seen Sir Michael Thelliston?"

"Not yet. He doesn't show up at dances. I shall meet him in the Row to-morrow morning. He's all right—a hero—a diplomat, a K.C.B. Write one of your little dainty notes to-night, ma'am, so that Lady Thelliston may get it at breakfast to-morrow."

There was no help for Lady Mary. Conrad fidgeted about the drawing-room till he had her seated at her Davenport, writing the invitation.

"I am giving her a choice of two days next week, and three days the week after."

"Thank you, ma'am. I think she'll choose the earliest, even if she throws over something good. She wants to have you for a friend."

"I don't think we can have an idea in common," said Lady Mary.

"Oh, but you can tell her about people, teach her how to steer her bark. A new-comer, an Anglo-Indian—what a privilege for such an one to know Lady Mary Harling."

His tone was a caress. He hung over his mother's chair, delighted at seeing the letter addressed and sealed. He rang for the servant to get it posted.

"At once, Thomas, and at the Post Office."

"You are going to ride with them to-morrow morning?" asked Lady Mary.

"To-morrow, and always, till they give me the cold shoulder. The General rides every day. It was only a chance that she was alone this morning. She rode on the north side of the Park to avoid the crowd."

"And you were with her all the time?"

"She would have found it difficult to shake me off."

He was not ashamed of his infatuation. It was young love, eager, headstrong, determined, Romeo's love for Juliet, after his heart had bled for Rosaline; a second love, ardent as the first, and perhaps no less fatal. To love like that, suddenly, unquestioning, was to strike the keynote of a tragedy.

Lady Mary was in a desperate pass. She could not openly oppose him by refusing to be friendly with these people. She must diplomatise, and still hope that the sudden fire would burn out quickly like a candle in a draught, wasting itself in a profligate flame.

With her son she must diplomatise; but with the sin-stained girl who had bewitched him she could deal plainly and speak straight words.

Her invitation was accepted promptly—for one of the earlier days. With a sinking heart she made up her party. A literary man and a soldier, the soldier young and attractive, would make the seventh and eighth of a friendly little dinner. Conrad was glad that they would be so few; and his mother hoped that her nephew, who was in the Scots Greys and a general favourite, might prove a counter attraction for Miss Thelliston, and perhaps develop that young lady's least winning characteristics. If, for instance, she were to show herself an incorrigible flirt, and so disgust Conrad in the dawn of love! Lady Mary's policy was Machiavelian and merciless. She felt that her cause was good, and fought without compunction.

The dinner was bright and gay, and Lady Mary's manœuvre was unsuccessful. Miss Thelliston's behaviour was perfect. While she was amiable to both young men she was familiar with neither, and she showed herself deeply interested in Daisy and in all womanly subjects, the pictures on the walls, the books on the tables, books fresh from the library, memoirs, letters, travels, philosophy, books that indicate the superior mind. In her tour of the rooms with Daisy after dinner, she ignored only one somewhat conspicuous object, Lady Mary's embroidery frame, where a solitary poplar showed amid a desert of tissue paper.

Sir Michael revealed himself to Lady Mary's anxious gaze as a person of sufficiently dignified aspect. He was considerably over six feet, very thin, and very upright; a hard man, with narrow steel-grey eyes, iron-grey hair cropped close, and a heavy moustache and beetling brows that were almost black. Lady Mary suspected a cruel mouth under that drooping moustache.

Had Miss Thelliston behaved badly, Lady Mary might have waited, still hoping that the danger would blow over, but seeing the girl's manners irreproachable she felt there was no time to be lost. Such a love-affair was like a quicksand, and Conrad was sinking so fast that he would soon be submerged beyond the hope of rescue. Whatever her power might be she must use it at once.

She invited Irene to her sofa with a smile, when the girl had made the round of the pictures and had said all that could be said about them.

"Please sit by my side for a few minutes, Miss Thelliston. I want to ask you something."

The delicate colour on the girl's cheek faded ever so slightly, and her eyes grew grave.

"Oh, I hope you are not going to be serious," she said in a very low voice. "Pray let bygones be bygones."

"I must be serious. I am not going to speak of the past, at least not more than is absolutely necessary. But I must speak to you about the future. Will you come to see me after your ride to-morrow morning, so that we may have half an hour's quiet talk together? Will you come to breakfast at half-past nine?"

"No, I won't break bread with you if you are going to talk seriously. I know what that means. I won't sit at table with you and Miss Meredith and your son, and pretend to be happy, if I have *that* on my mind. I'll come here at eleven o'clock, if you like. I am my own mistress till luncheon. Lady Thelliston requires the morning for her complexion."

"Then I shall expect you at eleven. Be assured I am not going to say anything unkind."

"I hope not, Lady Mary. I have had my fill of unkindness."

She rose and went over to the piano where Daisy was going to sing with Captain Mansfield, who was one of those young men who do things: singing, amateur acting, lightning portraits, tricks with billiard balls, and a little conjuring.

Professor Wilmer, the man of letters, walked to the other end of the room in disgust. In a friendly party of eight he ought to have been the star, and a monologue from him should have been the only entertainment; and here were an amateur tenor and contralto blocking conversation, and spoiling his evening.

The little Dresden clock on the mantel-shelf in Lady Mary's morning-room struck eleven, with a tiny silvery chime; the clock on the stairs solemnly repeated the information; and a church clock, ever so far away, sent the same message through the summer air, while Lady Mary moved about the room restlessly, nervous and apprehensive.

"Would the girl keep her appointment?"

She had only three minutes' uncertainty before the butler announced Miss Thelliston.

Irene was dressed simply and girlishly in a white frock and white hat with white gloves and sunshade. A small bunch of pink carnations at her waistband was the only touch of colour.

Her clothes would have been simple enough for a village in the heart of the country, but the general effect was distinguished, and her morning face was exquisite, her cheeks flushed with vivid rose, and her eyes brilliant as if with some great joy. It was not the countenance Lady Mary expected to see. Here there was no touch of shame or of remorse. Yet there was no defiance; only unmeasurable content.

"Will you sit here, by the window. We can talk quite at our ease. Daisy Meredith has gone for a walk with the dogs. I want to talk to you seriously, straight from my heart to your heart."

They were seated side by side on a large low sofa, that filled Lady Mary's favourite bow window, a window commanding a peep into Park Lane and the trees in Hamilton Gardens. There was a silence of some moments and then Mary Harling said gravely:

"I daresay you know that my son admires you, Miss Thelliston?"

"Yes, I know as much as that."

"It is only natural that he should admire a very beautiful girl, about whose antecedents he knows nothing; but I think your own good feeling, your own good taste, will induce you to do all in your power to discourage him?"

"But why, Lady Mary?"

"Need you ask me why? He is my son, my only son, dearer to me than life. Can't you understand that it would break my heart if he were to marry any woman upon whose girlhood there was a stain?"

"No, I can't understand. Have you forgotten your own words that last night on board the *Electra*? Some day, you said, a good man might want me for his wife; and you urged me to tell him my wretched story, and you told me that if he was indeed my true lover, he would forgive me, and take me to his heart, and cherish me for the rest of my days. That is what you told me, Lady Mary; so, now I suppose you wish me to tell your son the story of my life in Cashmere?"

"No, no, I want you to act like a true and generous woman, and to let my son go. His fancy has been caught by your beauty. There can be no depth or seriousness in his feeling for you. All you have to do is to let him see that you are not attracted by him, that he is nothing to you. It must be so easy for you to give up this one admirer, since you are lovely enough to have many suitors, men of high rank in the world, men who can give you a position that every other woman will envy."

"You are very kind to promise me such grand things, but I do not happen to care for them. Your son loves me with a most enchanting love, and I would rather be his wife than a duchess, if there were a duke in my horoscope."

"Oh, but you must not marry him—you must not. I won't live to see you married to my son," Lady Mary cried vehemently, losing all self-control.

"What will you do to prevent it? Everything was settled this morning, and I am engaged to your son. My father rode alone, for with this interview hanging over me I did not care for the Row. Conrad joined my father there, and told him that he wanted to marry me, and my father brought him home to breakfast, and after breakfast he followed me to the drawing-room. Oh, he is splendid, noble, generous, a king among men! I don't wonder you are proud of him. We were talking for a long time, heart to heart, and I promised to be his wife, and we were both as happy as mortal creatures can be. Are you going to try to part us? Will you break the oath you swore upon your crucifix—you, a good Christian? Will you tell him my story?"

"No, I can do nothing. It is you who must act. You have known him less than a month. You can't really love him."

"Juliet had not known Romeo half a dozen hours."

"Juliet! Juliet had not surrendered herself to a profligate, had not borne a profligate's child. Juliet was not a precocious sinner. I won't have you for my son's wife. Do you hear, Irene Thelliston? If I am tongue-tied, it is you who must disillusionise him. You must do everything that tact and cleverness can do to cure him of his infatuation without breaking his heart. That is what you have to do."

"And I am to marry any man I can catch, the highest in the land, so long as I don't marry your son?"

"You are not to marry my son. He has been deceived once, cruelly deceived by a girl he thought pure as snow. He has suffered. He shall not be deceived a second time. I will do anything—anything to save him from you!"

"Will you break your oath?"

"I don't know. I might be justified even in doing that, to save my son from dishonour. You think your secret is safely hidden; but I tell you no secret can be kept for ever—least of all the secret of a woman's shame. Some witness will rise up against you. The servant who brought you from India, your child—or the people who have the care of your child."

"My child only lived a few hours. I had been too unhappy to bring a new life into the world. My maid is in Australia. She is an honourable woman, after her lights, and she swore never to betray me. *She* will not break her oath."

"And your step-mother? Does not she know?"

"No one knows but my father. That's why we hate each other."

"Horrible!"

"Yes, it is horrible. I never look at him without shuddering at the thought of his contempt. In the midst of new friends who are kind enough to make much of me, I look across the crowd, and see his hard face, the face that has never looked at me kindly since I so sorely wanted a father's kindness. He—who has such need of pardon for his sins against my mother—cannot forgive me. I am a woman, and there is no pardon for a woman's sin."

"Your step-mother seems kind to you."

"Yes, she is kind, and I accept her kindness. There are compromises. I live under the same roof with her, though she helped to break my mother's heart. I don't mean that she was my father's mistress. I should draw the line at that. But I know that she flirted with him, and kept him dangling about her when all his time and care ought to have been given to his dying wife."

"You must be very unhappy in such a home."

"We don't say too much about home. My father and his wife have made me understand that I am expected to marry before the end of the season. She buys me nice clothes, and he has given me her horse for the Park. The clothes and the horse are to get me a husband. Even that slip of a house is more than my father can comfortably afford. He would be better off in Ireland. I am to marry—and to marry well. He is enchanted with your son's offer."

"Your father is a man of the world. Does he think your Cashmere escapade will never come to light?"

Lady Mary's irritation had got the better of her womanly feeling. For the moment she was merciless.

"Yes. I have no doubt my father believes—as I do—that Fate will not be so cruel as to hurt me any more."

"And your lover—the wretch who seduced and deserted you? Is he dead?"

"I have never heard of his death."

"Suppose you were to meet him by and by, as the wife of a man of position. Don't you think that would be rather awkward for you and for your husband?"

"I think not. He showed himself a man of the world when he went away, and made no sign if we were to meet—he would show himself a man of the world again. I have no fear that he would betray me."

"Or that he would make love to you? And how about your own feelings? You must have loved him desperately when—when you let him spoil your life."

"You have no right to talk to me like that," cried the girl, with sudden vehemence. "What do you know of such tragedies—you with your smooth existence, hedged round with conventionalities, guarded on every side, you who could hardly have gone wrong if you had been the most vicious of women? What do you know about me? When I let him spoil my life! you say—When I let him! I was seventeen—and I had been educated by the proper people who never hint that life has dangers. When I let him! I was in the power of a profligate, intoxicated with sweet words, with flattered vanity, told for the first time that I was beautiful, and that I was beloved. What did I know of love but the sweetness of it—the love I had read about in Romeo and Juliet—the love *he* read of—the love of Haidee for Juan—oh, so overpoweringly sweet in the ears of ignorance. You don't know—you can never, never, never understand!"—

"Yes, I think I can. I am sorry for you. I blame your seducer, and the woman who left you in his power; the wicked woman who had the fate of a girl in her keeping, and took no care. I have always been sorry for you—but I will not let my son marry you."

"But you promised me a husband; some good man who would hear my confession and pity me, and take me to his heart. What kind of a man was he to be? A village schoolmaster, perhaps, or a curate, a shopkeeper's son who had won a scholarship and got himself ordained. Someone second-class."

"You shall not marry my son."

"How will you hinder me?"

"By every means in my power—and you may be sure a mother's intelligence will find the way—though I may not see it now. You shall not marry him. I could tell you something about him—that would scare you, perhaps, and make you glad to give him up."

"You would tell me that seven years of his young life were wasted in a madhouse. Do you think that would frighten me?"

"How did you know?"

"He told me this morning, before he asked me to be his wife. Perhaps even you don't know how noble he is—how frank, and chivalrous, and true—a king among men. And can you think that I will give him up? I have suffered by a man's wickedness, I have drained the cup of sorrow and shame. I live with a father I hate, and a step-mother I despise. And when a good man comes to me and offers me a love that leapt into life the night we met, strangers in one hour, lovers in the next, do you think that I am going to let my true love go?"

"If you have any sense of honour you cannot marry him."

"But I might marry the other man—the curate—or the school-master? Remember what you said to me. I had only to tell him my story. If the worst comes to the worst I can tell Conrad."

"And you think he would forgive you?"

"I am sure he would. I should make him very miserable; it would be a cruel thing to do. It would take the bloom off our love and our happiness; but he would not send me away. I have grown into his heart. He could not do without me."

She had calmed herself after her burst of passion, and her face grew radiant as she spoke of her lover. She paused before the mantelpiece for a moment or two, while she adjusted her hat, and smiled at the brilliant reflection.

"He loves me, Lady Mary, and I can make him happy," she said.

"You had better be kind. Let the dead bury their dead. Just take time, and think things over quietly."

She moved towards the door, while Lady Mary stood with an adamantine countenance and forgot even to ring the bell. She held out her hand at parting, but Lady Mary would not take it.

Half-way downstairs she met Conrad, who caught her in his arms, surprised and rapturous.

"My angel! You have been with my mother? You have told her? I was just going to her. How sweet of you!—She ought to be delighted."

"She is hardly that—as yet. It is so sudden—so dreadfully quick —for a mother. But she will be pleased by and by, when she knows me better. I am going to make you happy, Conrad, oh, so happy!"

She let her head sink upon his breast, half swooning in the sudden reaction from the scene above stairs, and he smothered her face with kisses, and had no memory of a face almost as lovely that had nestled there and been kissed as fondly by a passionate lad of twenty, eight years ago.

When does the new love remember the old?

They had the spacious landing all to themselves just long enough for this little love scene, in the shelter of tall palms and the cool light filtered through Venetian shutters; and then an electric bell rang sharply, the servants were on the alert in the hall below, and Conrad had to behave with circumspection as he escorted his sweetheart to the door and went out with her. That she should walk alone to Chapel Street, that radiant creature whose dazzling beauty challenged every eye, would have been out of the question. He went with her, and they made a detour by Park Lane and Green Street, and they talked, as only newly-plighted lovers can, of a future of ineffable bliss.

CHAPTER VIII

MARY HARLING was beaten. She had the ever-present memory of what the doctors had said to her, that grave warning of peril; and, with the revelation of her son's impassioned temperament which every day was brought more vividly before her mind, she could hardly question the medical verdict. This fine brain was too nearly allied with the heart to stand the shock of an unhappy love. The same kind of trouble that had been fatal to him in his twentieth year might again be fatal; since in every characteristic, in every feeling and impulse he seemed no older at eight-and-twenty than he had been as an undergraduate. It might be that those years at Roehampton counted for nothing, and that he was still in the dawn of manhood, eager and impetuous, seeking the blue flower of joy with a fervour that would not brook disappointment.

Lady Mary felt that her armoury was exhausted. She had used her strongest weapons, and her sword had bent in her hand, her gun had missed fire. The girl had met threats and entreaties with the same indomitable spirit. The girl meant to marry her son. No hope remained but in Machiavelian tactics, and Lady Mary felt that she must take things quietly, and exert her utmost power of Machiavelianism.

Conrad's light foot came bounding up the stair while she still sat before her writing-table disconsolate, just as she had sunk down when the girl left her. He dashed into the room, bringing the breath of summer and youth and happiness with him.

"My dear, dear mother! She has told you! She came herself to tell you. Could anything be sweeter? Of course she must adore you. She who has no real mother. You are not going to lose a son. You are going to gain a daughter."

He was on his knees by her chair; he had seized her cold hand and was kissing it, in a fever of filial love.

"Dear mother, tell me you are pleased."

Ah, what a struggle it cost, the wan smile, the low murmur.

84

"I must be content, if my dear son is happy."

"And would you not have chosen her? Is she not all you would have chosen?"

"I have no choice. I have never thought of choosing. I only wanted my dearest to be happy."

"And I am going to be happy, divinely happy. I feel as if this earth I tread on had been changed to an Olympian cloud. I walk on air! I am breathless in a rarefied atmosphere. Think what it is to me, mother, to find this pure and perfect pearl—after the disillusion of my youth—when my goddess, my angel, the creature I almost worshipped, was shown to me in a moment—without a note of warning—as the most worthless of her sex—a hypocrite and a liar—a prize-fighter's light o' love! Can you wonder that my mind gave way under the shock?"

There was a silence, while Conrad still knelt, his mother's head bent over him, her arms about his neck.

Oh, the agony of it; to know that he was again deceived, that this new angel who brought him ineffable bliss was a mock angel, and that at any moment the mask might drop, and he might know himself again the dupe of secondhand charms. To know this, and to be unable to undeceive him, constrained to silence by so dreadful a fear!

Her oath might perhaps have been as nothing to her—the sin of perjury might have lain lightly on her conscience—had it been for his interest to tell him the cruel truth. But she could not speak words that would crush him in the dawn of joy, at the risk of a shattered mind and a life ruined for ever. Better that he should be happy in his own way, perhaps never to be undeceived. It might be, as the girl said, that no witness would ever rise up against her; and it might be that she loved Conrad as he deserved to be loved. She who had so suffered might love better than the sinless and the untried. Her affection ought to be so much the stronger for her gratitude to him who taught her the divinity of a good man's love.

"Mother, you are crying! Is that the way you welcome joyful news?"

"My dearest, there are always two sides to a question. I want you to be happy—but we have been all the world to each other, you and I. You must allow something for a mother's jealousy. And then I have been thinking of Daisy—poor Daisy!"

"Why poor? Daisy and Irene will be capital friends. We shall take Daisy about with us on the motor. Daisy will have a good time doing gooseberry."

"Will it be quite a good time, do you think? To be a third, and rather in the way, after the long rides with you in Hampshire, the croquet, the billiards, the time when you devoted yourself to her all day long, so that I almost thought——"

"You almost thought I was falling in love with her—and I thought so too, ma'am, and one day—one heavenly May morning when the world seemed enchanted—I was on the brink of a proposal. We had ridden to the edge of the Forest, we were in that lonely wood, you know, in the valley beyond Ringwood, and I felt like a man under a spell. I was almost drunk with the rapture of life in that green woodland, under that azure sky—and Daisy seemed the spirit of the wood, a most enchanting hamadryad* in a neat little riding habit. I was nearly gone when I remembered that *au fond** my feelings were simply cousinly, or even brotherly—and that no doubt Daisy had just the same temperate affection for me."

"I am not so sure of that, Conrad. I am afraid your kindness in those happy days at Cranford may have turned her head a little. She is very sensitive."

"And she is six-and-twenty—heads don't spin round easily at that age—and it is only a mother who believes that every girl in the world must find her son irresistible. Daisy and I are comrades and friends, and always will be, if she takes to Irene; as I feel sure she will."

"My dearest," and again there were signs of tears.

"Oh, mother, why this dolefulness? Is not my love a lady, the daughter of a man who has fought for his country, and won his Sovereign's recognition? Is not my love fair?"

"Too fair, too fair! Oh, Conrad, can't you understand that I am fearful of a love that is founded only upon beauty. It fills me with fear when I see my son the slave of a lovely face. What do you know of Miss Thelliston except that she is beautiful? Your father and I had known each other for more than a year before he asked me to marry him. I knew all about him—his conduct—his opinions—his religion. I knew that I was giving myself to a man who would never disappoint me, who would be husband, friend, counsellor, all the world to me; as he was, till death took him."

The rush of tears that came after those words seemed natural, and Conrad was not offended.

"Dearest of mothers, yours was an ideal courtship in the old-fashioned jog-trot way. But I belong to a swifter-moving generation, and I yearn for the poetry of life. Remember how your favourite Shakespeare said, 'He never loved that loved not at first sight.'* I have no doubt that my father was in love with you all that year of your acquaintance, though he was not so impetuous as I am. Come now, ma'am, let us all be happy. Open your heart to my sweet love, and every day will make you fonder of her. By the by, why didn't you ask her to come back to luncheon? She wouldn't come for my asking."

"I didn't think of it."

"Oh, but you must make her welcome, ma'am, you must make her feel that she belongs to us, and that she is not to stand upon punctilio. I don't. I told her to tell Lady Thelliston that I was going to lunch with them, and, by Jove if it's twenty minutes past one, and they lunch at half-past."

Conrad got up, shook himself, like a dog in good spirits, and was at the door when his mother asked:

"Are you going anywhere this afternoon?"

"To Richmond on the Mercedes. Tell Daisy to be ready at a quarter to four. We shall have tea at the 'Star.' Will you drive down and join us?"

"No, dear, it's too far."

"We shall be back in time for a stroll in the Park. I shall expect to find you there."

He was gone—gone to the new love and the new life. Come what might, no word nor act of hers must bring about the ruin of his hopes.

Henceforward Conrad's courtship went on velvet. Everybody seemed to rejoice in the joy of these young lovers, since the two persons to whom that sudden betrothal brought pain instead of joy had to smooth their brows and to hide a stricken heart with a smile. It was only when Conrad told Daisy Meredith of his engagement, and entreated her warmest regard for his future wife, that she knew how dear he had become to her, or the dream she had cherished that she had become dear to him.

Conrad had been so kind, so cruelly, so fatally kind in those glad days at Cranford. He had seemed so completely content with life in her society, while every day had brought them some new discovery of mutual tastes, opinions, sympathies, from trivial things, the love of a dog, a horse, a flower, or some particular phase in the sky, the earth, the atmosphere, to the highest, the deeply-felt need of a Personal God, the anxious belief in the Hereafter.

In a moment that dream had vanished. He might still be her friend. In telling her of his new happiness he had dwelt upon his affection for her, had urged her to be to his wife as a sister. But he could never more be as he had been in that golden Maytime, the blossoming season of her life, the season in which life had been more than life, and earth had ceased to be earthy.

Not for worlds would she have appeared disappointed or forlorn. She had that fine feminine pluck which can look upon the funeral pyre of love and smile. She played her poor little part of gooseberry with grace and vivacity. She was never in the way, and never out of the way when wanted. She suffered the rush and noise of the Mercedes, the dust of the roads, the monotony of afternoon teas, that whether at Richmond, or Esher, or Wimbledon, or Windsor, were always the image of each other.

She talked when she was wanted to talk, and was always absorbed in the landscape when the lovers began to whisper confidences, those mysterious confidences which engaged young men and maidens have to impart to each other. She did all that the situation demanded, with a face that beamed with intelligence, and a heart heavier than lead. The shabby house at Holloway, the bickering parents, the slovenly parlourmaid, would have seemed a haven of peace, but she was too proud to fly. Someone might get an inkling of her secret, if she were to show the faintest distaste for her sickening office. Happily for her there was a limit to her martyrdom, for the wedding was to take place in August; Sir Michael and his future son-in-law being of one opinion as to the needlessness of delay, while Irene had consented readily to an early marriage.

"If we were to be engaged for years I could not trust you more than I do now," she told her lover. "I know how good you are. I know how happy we are going to be."

That was the song she sang to him in all those joyous days. They were going to be happy. She was going to make him happy. It was the string she harped upon on love's mystical lyre.

Material arrangements are easy when the suitor has thirty thousand a year. Lady Mary insisted upon giving up Cranford; but she would of course retain the house in Hertford Street, which was hers for life. Conrad and Irene had the joy of house-hunting among their other pleasures; and house-hunting, when rent is no object, is as joyous a business as it is weary and wearing for small purses. Even in this Daisy had to assist, scaling four-storey staircases in Hill Street and Charles Street, and Green Street, and Norfolk Street, till after days of exploration a small house was discovered in Park Lane, which was the situation Irene had desired from the first.

After the discovery of the ideal house there came consultations and fierce discussions with the ideal architect—that is to say, the architect at the top of the mode that season, who was something of an autocrat, and wanted his own way about every detail; so that at last Conrad had to remind him that it was he and his wife who would have to live in the house, and that however perfect it might be as a work of art, it would be hard lines if they did not like it.

When, however, this famous artist sent in drawings of the house as it was to be after he had worked his will upon it, the blue windows and pale pink walls, and delicate touches of water-colour, had such a Ruskinesque effect* that Irene was all for letting the architect have a free hand, and finally it was agreed that he should alter and bedevil the house, until nothing but the mere shell of the original structure would remain, that which had been kitchen becoming wine-cellar, and servants' bedrooms being transformed into kitchens, all inner walls on the first and second floor being removed, leaving vast spaces where there had been small rooms, and ceilings supported by steel girders and a pilaster or two.

Daisy told Lady Mary that she liked the original telescopic drawing-rooms better, the positive, comparative, and superlative, expanding from a boudoir not much bigger than a powder closet at the back of the house, through a smallish middle room, to a somewhat spacious drawing-room with three French windows opening on a balcony. The Early Victorian balcony was to disappear, and the three windows were to become one, stone-mullioned, mediæval, with a deep window seat, and leaded casements to let in the rain. There was to be nothing more recent than the period of Francis the First and Diane de Poictiers.

This transmogrification would take time, and the house would not be ready till next season.

Sir Michael and Lady Thelliston went to Hampshire in the Panhard with the lovers, to see the place which was to be their daughter's country home; and all things were admired and approved. Irene had not Daisy's way of looking at horses and dogs, nor did she walk straight into the hearts of the Irish setters, as Daisy had done; but she admired the fine old quadrangle of red brick and stone, where stables and saddle-rooms, and coach-houses and grooms' quarters were dignified by the spaciousness of the enclosure, and the stone basin round which the pigeons clustered, where there had been a fountain that had not played within the memory of man. She admired the large rooms, the broad oak balusters and carved newels of the staircase, the grandeur and spaciousness everywhere.

"Is this really to be my house?" she said, with a glad little laugh that Conrad thought enchanting.

They lunched in the large dining-room where the round table looked like an island in an ocean of Turkey carpet. They were a cosy party of four, Daisy not being required on this occasion; and it mattered nothing to Conrad that his future father-in-law had a cold, cruel face, or that his future mother-in-law's complexion was a curious and instructive spectacle in the clear light of a July noontide. Conrad knew nothing, he cared for nothing, save the girl by whose side he was sitting, and whose slender grace as she moved about the rooms that were to be her own had enthralled him. They had roamed over the house, hand in hand, exploring rooms and corridors, looking at family portraits, from Lawrence to Buckner,* the first Harling of any importance having been painted by the former master.

"Ours isn't a long pedigree," Conrad said, laughing. "We only date from Sir Thomas Lawrence."

"Ah, but on your mother's side."

"Oh, the Duke's family tree begins with King Stephen's armour-bearer, and the family is as rusty as the armour that hangs in the Castle hall."

Irene was enthusiastic about the billiard-room and library, with a door of communication.

"I shall sit here and read after dinner, while you and your friends play," she said, looking at the shelves, where every book she had ever heard of or desired seemed to be waiting for her, books having been one of Mr. Harling's vanities, exquisite books in exquisite bindings.

The trousseau was a business that occupied many mornings. Sir Michael being too much a man of the world to hold his hand when his daughter was marrying thirty thousand a year, and when her settlement was to be exceptionally generous, nothing asked from the bride's people and everything given. Irene herself showed indifference about her wedding clothes, rare in any young woman, rarer perhaps in an old woman. She allowed her step-mother and the dressmaker to choose and settle everything, only stipulating that most of her frocks should be white, and that her trousseau should be planned with a view to foreign travel rather than to display at home.

"We shall be wandering about the world till next season," she told Madame Herminie, "and I shall go to any queer wild places my husband wants to see; so you must give me no useless finery." But when the suave and expensive Herminie heard of a winter in Egypt, she protested that madam would want more evening frocks and smarter evening coats than if she were staying in London.

Irene shrugged her shoulders disdainfully.

"I am not going to parties at huge hotels," she said. "I am going to live in a felucca* or under canvas with my husband."

My husband! The word charmed her. She had never dreamed of this joyous love, never hoped to be so honoured and so cherished, she who had suffered the dull despair of a young life that has no fair outlook. Fate had been good to her after all.

Only one thing troubled Conrad in this joyous time, and that was a certain want of cordiality between his mother and the girl of his heart. In vulgar parlance, these two whom he loved best in the world did not take to each other.

Lady Mary was courteous, and Irene was unfailing in all proper marks of respect for the lady's age and position; but there were no signs of growing intimacy, still less of affection.

"I thought you would be so fond of my mother," he said one day, with almost a note of reproach.

"I shall be fond of her when she is fond of me," Irene answered, "but that has to come. Perhaps when we have been married a year or two, and I have made you happy, the ice will melt."

"Women are inscrutable. I made sure that you would love each other. She never had a daughter, and you who loved your mother so dearly——"

"Dearly, dearly, dearly. Don't speak of her. Don't make me think of her, and her last days upon this earth, when I counted every breath she drew, hung upon every word—faint words—at long intervals—and when I knew that each word might be the last."

He caught her to his heart. He kissed away her tears. Never, never would he again invoke a memory that grieved her.

"My mother will adore you by and by," he said, and then in a lower voice he asked: "Can you guess when she will love you best?"

He whispered the answer to his own question. "When our first-born child is laid in her arms."

Irene's head drooped lower on his breast, and the lips that were hidden from him were mute. She clung to him in silence, and he felt the hurried beating of her heart, and knew he had distressed her, but could not understand why.

Conrad never spoke to her again about her relations with his mother, comforting himself with the assurance that intimacy and affection would come in good time. Irene had spoken words of wisdom. His mother would love the woman who gave happiness to her son. Perhaps such close relations must always begin with a little aversion, or at least with some distrust.

After her terrible interview with Lady Mary, Irene had resolved never to bend her neck before a woman who had so outraged her pride of womanhood. Whatever love or kindness was to come in the future it should come unsought. She would never plead *in formâ pauperis*, never take the lower ground of acknowledged guilt. Strong in Conrad's love she would defy the world. She had brought her father to her feet, after years of unkindness. He fawned upon her, he praised and admired her, and made believe that no cloud had ever crossed her sky. He even talked freely before Conrad of her life in Ireland, hidden in a rustic village, with an aunt who worshipped her. Nobody had ever told him of any such worship. The idea was spontaneous.

Lady Mary wondered at the girl's calm front, and perhaps, in her heart of hearts, admired her for being so quietly defiant, so self-assured and resolute. The calmness under deeply agitating conditions indicated good blood, was indeed as much a sign and token of race as her small feet and delicate hands, and all those other marks of refinement in her beautiful person. A girl of mean birth would have trembled and cringed.

And so the summer days went by, fleet and sweet as summer days can be when people are ineffably happy. The lovers were rarely parted between early morning in the Row and the small hours after a ball, except in the inevitable time which the least vain of young women must sacrifice to the exigencies of London clothes. First came the morning ride, and after breakfast a walk or shopping; and then luncheon in Chapel Street, or perhaps one of Lady Mary's luncheon parties, which she could not desist from giving all at once. She had, indeed, to do more entertaining now that her son was engaged to be married.

In the afternoons there were long jaunts in one of the motors, and on opera nights there was an early dinner in Hertford Street, and an evening in Lady Mary's capacious box; and there were occasional dinner parties, and dances almost every night, dances to which the pretty Miss Thelliston was always bidden, dances with chaperons, and friendly little dances without chaperons, so that scarcely a night passed in that enchanting July when Conrad's arms were not encircling his betrothed in the waltz they both loved, and in which they both excelled.

Then there were the suburban races, Sandown and Kempton, to which Conrad carried Irene and his cousin, with some agreeable youth or middle-aged swain to make a fourth and amuse Daisy. Captain Mansfeld was the favourite, as he was keen on racing and knew the lineage and previous performances of every horse, and the merits and peculiarities of every jockey.

It was one Saturday afternoon at Sandown, under tropical sunshine, in the mob of overpowering frocks and hats, and more or less attractive faces, that they met a man who had achieved a momentary distinction by the purchase of a famous Derby winner, and by the success of one of his own horses at the Newmarket First Spring meeting. He had a horse running at Sandown this afternoon, and had that peculiar air of suppressed agitation common to owners when their luck trembles in the balance, and in this condition, with eyes brightened as with fever, and a certain over-alertness of movement and manner, he ran against Captain Mansfeld, who was walking with Daisy Meredith, while Conrad and Irene sauntered after them. It was still early in the afternoon, and the most important race was yet to come.

The man had a loud voice, resonant, and not unmelodious, and they could hear every word as they approached. It was all about his horse, and the chances for and against.

He was a large man, tall and broad-shouldered, handsome, commanding of aspect, a man who looked as if he had once been a soldier, well set up still, but a little out of training. Idleness and high living had set their mark upon the magnificent figure, and the face was one upon which high thinking had never been expressed. It was perfect from the sculptor's point of view, but the beauty was purely physical, the type suggestive of the arena and not of the forum.

"Come round and look at Horoscope before they saddle him: if Miss Meredith is fond of horses she'll appreciate his good looks," he was saying, having in a manner forced Mansfeld to introduce him to the young lady; and then as Conrad and his sweetheart approached, he turned and met them face to face.

He looked at Irene with a surprise that was instantaneous, and then with an expectant look that obliged her to recognise him. She bowed ever so slightly, and walked on, quickening her pace, with her large white sunshade lowered a little, so that her face was hidden.

"Do you know that man?" asked Conrad, with a lover's jealous distrust of any stranger who presumes to claim acquaintance with the beloved.

"I met him years ago in India."

"Is he a friend of Sir Michael's?"

"No. I don't think my father knows him."

"But you met him?"

"It was in Cashmere; he was a friend of my cousin's."

"Was he in the army?"

"Yes, he was in the Grenadiers.* But he had left the army and was travelling—for his amusement."

"Wouldn't have him in the Guards perhaps; he doesn't look their sort."

"What is the matter with him?"

"Something indefinite—something I don't want to put into plain words. Some men are born so, men whose blood is of the deepest blue, and whose ancestors were fine gentlemen in the first Crusade."

"You condemn him on rather slight evidence—never having even talked to him."

"I heard him talk just now; bragging about his horse, wanting my cousin to go and look at the brute. Out of his own mouth he has condemned himself."

"I'm sorry your cousin had to suffer the burden of his acquaintance."

There had been no change in Irene's voice or manner as she talked of the man, not the faintest sign of fear or distress; yet this chance meeting was one of the dark moments of life. She felt the hand of fate upon her. She had hugged herself with the assurance that she would never see that face again, never hear again the voice that had once charmed her. To-day she saw him as Conrad saw him—with a deep disgust. Handsome? Yes! Splendid as common clay unillumined by soul can be—an earth-man, in whom there was no sign of the immortal mind.

She wondered if he had changed utterly from the man she had once loved—the man to whom she gave her childish admiration, her childish trust, the man who had pursued her with a passionate insistence from the hour when her eyes first looked up at him with a schoolgirl's innocent admiration of a magnificent being, the typical Guardsman of the romantic novel.

She had been able to control voice and manner, but she could not command her colour; and presently when they were sitting at tea, and she could no longer shelter herself under her parasol, Conrad exclaimed at her pallor. She had been walking in the sun. It was his fault. He was as much distressed as if he had taken her unawares through a plague-stricken city. He was sure that her head ached, that she was almost fainting. All her protestations to the contrary were useless.

He looked appealingly at Daisy. What had better to be done? Should they go home directly after tea? Perhaps he could find a doctor who would prescribe something. He could run to a chemist at Esher to get a prescription made up. He looked as troubled as if death were in the air.

Irene protested that she had no headache.

"Please let us sit quietly somewhere, out of the sun. That is all I want. Perhaps Daisy will sit with me in some shady corner while you and Captain Mansfeld look at the race."

"As if I should leave you!" cried Conrad reproachfully.

"I give you my word I am not going to die," said Irene, with a silvery laugh that was reassuring.

He told Mansfeld and Daisy to go and amuse themselves, and to be at the gate ready for the drive home, at a quarter to seven; and then he went off with Irene, away from the race-course and the crowd, to stroll on Esher Common.

It was Irene who suggested the Common.

"It will be a relief to be away from all those frocks and hats," she said, "if you don't mind not seeing the race."

"As if I should mind; as if I wanted to see anything in the world except your face! When that looks pale and wan my world collapses. You gave me a scare just now, Irene; but a little bit of pink has come back; just the ghost of your morning colour, when we meet in the Park and I say to myself: here comes my rose of June."

They were to dine at Hertford Street at half-past seven, as it was an opera night, *Don Giovanni*, the old music they both adored, having that uneducated love of music which must be sustained with melody.

Irene was in beauty again when they met the other two at the gate.

"A pity you lost the race," said Mansfeld. "There was some fine riding, and Middlemore's horse won by half a length."

"Middlemore?"

"The owner of the favourite. The man who was talking to me when you and Miss Thelliston joined us."

"Oh, is that his name? Irene knew him in Cashmere; at least, he was an acquaintance of her cousin's. Not a very desirable acquaintance, I should think. But if he's a friend of yours I've nothing to say against him."

"I don't think there is anything to be said against him—except that he wasn't popular in his regiment. His father was a manufacturer somewhere in the north—and Middlemore had plenty of money when he was in the regiment, and I believe he spent it royally."

"But if his money is gone how does he come by a racing stable?"

"Oh, his father is rich enough to keep him going. He's an only son, and he married an American girl—a millionaire's orphan daughter from Boston, very refined and nice—but not handsome."

"Was she with him to-day?"

"No. She crossed the Atlantic in her coffin last March—to lie in the family vault with her New England ancestors."

This was while they waited for the motor. There was not much more talk after they had taken their seats, and Conrad had his mind and his hands occupied in steering through the crowd of carriage people who hated motors, and motor people who hated other motors; no time for more than an occasional word to the two girls sitting behind him, muffled in their white cloaks and veils, no opportunity for any confidences till the Mercedes stopped before the white door in Chapel Street and Irene alighted.

"Only a quarter of an hour to dress," said Conrad, as he handed her out. "I shall send the motor back for you."

"Please don't trouble. I can have a cab."

"Too slow. My mother is a dragon of punctuality."

Irene was nearly as white as her chiffon frock when she appeared in Lady Mary's drawing-room—and again Conrad protested that it was his fault for having kept her on the lawn in the glaring sunshine. She had struggled against that deadly faintness during her hurried toilet, the maid doing everything that her own active hands usually did, and dressing her as if she had been a doll. She dared not look at herself in the glass. A great dread had come upon her since she had known that Henry Middlemore was free.

She talked gaily enough to satisfy her lover while they were at dinner, and afterwards at the opera when the curtain was down. Him she might deceive, but she saw Lady Mary watching her with an uneasy expression. She who was in the secret of the past no doubt divined that a worse trouble than a walk in the afternoon sun had blanched that perfect face. Happily there was no dance that Saturday night, nowhere to go after the opera, which was over early. Sir Michael and his wife were dining out, and had not come home when Lady Mary's landau* brought Irene to her door, and her lover murmured his last fond words at parting.

"No Row to-morrow; but you would not be well enough to ride if it were a lawful day. I shall call early to ask about you—but you mustn't come down to breakfast or go and sit in a stifling church. If you have rested and are well enough for a stroll in Hamilton Gardens at one o'clock, I will get my aunt's key. You shan't be stared at and pointed at in the Park."

"Pray don't keep Lady Mary waiting."

She was glad when the door closed upon him. His tenderness

could not comfort her. All around her was dark. She felt as if she had suddenly become blind, and must grope her way among unknown obstacles.

There was a letter lying on the hall-table, a thick letter with a large staring scarlet seal, like a gout of blood, she thought.

The servant picked it up and carried it to her on a salver, as she went towards the staircase.

"A messenger brought it, ma'am, after ten o'clock."

She had divined, without seeing the address, that it was for her.

A carriage stopped at the door as she ran upstairs, and she heard her father's voice in the hall before she could get into her room. The dinner party had been later than usual, and no one but the servants had seen the letter. She locked her door to keep out the French maid who was Lady Thelliston's servant, and who had very little respite from her assistance in those elaborate arts which maintain fictitious beauty. What scanty leisure she had was at Miss Thelliston's service, and she was called a joint maid.

Irene switched on the light and flung herself into a chair by the open window to read her letter. She knew the hand, too well, too well. How many surreptitious scraps of notes had been secretly delivered—in her book—in her fan—in the loop of a sash—in a bunch of tropical flowers? Dear, dear letters they had been to her in those foolish days, before the knowledge of evil. Letters telling her she had looked lovelier than ever at the ball last night—had danced divinely—in a word that she was adorable.

"Oh, that delicious pink frock! You were like Venus in a rosy cloud. I think there is something of that sort in Virgil."

Adorable, adorable, adorable! The scraps of bold manly writing all sang the same song: all told her she was lovely and beloved, and all pleaded for more intimate moments—a walk in the compound in the moonlight—a *tête-à-tête* ride—some sweet solitude of two that was to be managed somehow; some evasion of her chaperon, some escape from the crowd. His brain was fertile in expedients. He was always telling her how to elude the people whose duty it was to take care of her, always teaching her how to deceive.

Those little scraps of praise and love had been very dear, for it was thrilling to the inexperienced girl to know herself the central point of a strong man's thoughts, the absorbing interest of his life—to be told of sleepless nights spent in thinking of her, of days that were pain and grief because they had to be spent away from her.

And now the same strong penmanship was a thing of horror, a thing that recalled the folly, the degradation of that miserable past.

Every word in that long letter was like a drop of molten lead, for to her the letter might mean doom.

"MY DARLING,

"I have spent a weary hour hunting for your address. The beautiful Miss Thelliston! That's what people call you. I had heard of the beautiful Miss Thelliston; but I had actually forgotten your surname, and it never occurred to me that this much-admired she was my Haidee, my child-wife, the only girl I ever loved with the whole force and passion of my soul. Ah, dearest child, you cannot have forgotten the night when I lay at your feet, and would have gladly died there rather than take up the burden of life with another woman.

"But I had to take up my burden. The fragile creature to whom I had pledged myself would have died if I had forsaken her. Those who knew her best, the aunt who had brought her up, the cousin who was like a sister, had warned me that to her sensitive nature disillusion would be fatal. It was not her fortune that tempted me, for my expectations from my father made me careless of that.

"I had to choose between my divine girl and the woman older than me by a year, who believed in me and depended upon me for the happiness of her life. Irene would soon forget the romantic dream of an Indian summer, a fairy tale of the hills and rose gardens; but my Boston sweetheart would not forget. She had given me the deep love of a thoughtful self-contained woman. I could not cheat her.

"She was a dear and devoted wife, and I think she was happy with me. She never knew that she was not the first and only woman who had ever held my heart. She died in my arms after a year of troubled health, during which I did everything that care and science could do to keep her alive. She left me rich and childless, free to begin life again—but with very little interest in anything except my racing stud—which had amused and pleased her—and in a rubber at Bridge.

"Then in a moment your face flashed upon me, and I knew that life was worth living. I am free, dearest, I am a free man now. The times are changed since that day when I stood before your cousin feeling like a beaten hound, pretending that I had thought of you only as an enchanting child, the sweet companion of an idle day—you—you—the girl I adored, my Haidee, my bride! Well, it was hard lines for us both; but we have a long life of happiness waiting for us, a life that will make amends. You are still in the dawn of girlhood, very little older than in those wild days, and ever so much lovelier. I am not by any means an old fogey, and to have you for my own will make me young again.

"Dearest, let it be soon. Every day will seem an age till I have you in my arms, my own till death. We can be married quietly, and just slip away to Italy on our way to India, and that romantic valley where we met. Think how delicious it would be to revisit the place where we were so happy, to wander once again in those enchanting scenes where we first knew the rapture of mutual love.

"For my own part I think it will save all troublesome explanations if we keep everything dark till after we are safely married, and have left England. You can meet me in the Park some morning, and we can be married by special license at the least frequented church in your parish; but if, on the other hand, you prefer to tell your father that you are going to marry me, having known and liked me years ago as a chance acquaintance in Cashmere, he will naturally inquire about my means. In that case you can tell him I can afford to make a liberal settlement, and that I feel sure I can satisfy him. My wife left me all her fortune, including her property in Yorkshire—an estate bought soon after our marriage—big farms and substantial homesteads, a fine park and a picturesque Jacobean house, which I know my Irene will love—as she will love the horses that have been my one extravagance of late years. But my bright bird shall never be caged in her country home an hour longer than she is supremely happy there. She shall have all the world to roam over at her own sweet will, with a husband whose delight will be to please her. Let me have a letter to-morrow morning by a messenger. This hotel is not half a mile from your house.

"Your devoted

"HAL.

"Saturday night.
"The Carlton Hotel."

This was his letter. This was the offer that he made in good faith, never for a moment doubting her acceptance. She belonged to him by that shameful past, that past of which he could write so lightly, having known only the sweetness of it. One bad half hour with her chaperon; one passionate outbreak of remorse, in the dead of the Indian night; just a few curses and groans and tears; and his price had been paid. He loved and he rode away. The light love was forgotten perhaps, and had only revived at sight of her, a new fancy, selfish, impetuous, as the old passion.

And her year of ignominy and suffering, that unhappy time in which she hardly dared to lift her eyes before the few people who came to her aunt's house, the priest, the parson, the hunting squire and his wife and daughters. Her aunt's friends were not many; but she hated them all. Her pride grew fiercer in that secret humiliation. No one knew, no one was ever to know! Her aunt, Mrs. Fitzpatrick, was a resolute managing woman, but not unkind, not without compassion. The youth of the victim weighed with her. The father had thought chiefly, or solely, of the disgrace, the trouble, and inconvenience for himself. His sister could pity the girl whose innocence had been the cause of her fall.

Irene's health had broken down soon after her arrival in Ireland, and she had been ill enough to be kept in seclusion, waited on and nursed by her aunt, till the hour of her trial drew near, and then aunt and niece went unattended to an obscure sea-side village in the West, more than a hundred miles from Mrs. Fitzpatrick's home; and here, though the aunt gave her own name, the niece was described as Mrs. Brown, whose husband was soldiering in India.

Mrs. Fitzpatrick's air of impeccable respectability, a certain authoritativeness that argued social status, left no room for question. The landlady was delighted to have such lodgers at the end of the season, when her usual tenants were gone.

To-night, sitting with her hands clasped above her head, and Henry Middlemore's letter before her, Irene lived over that dreadful time. Imagination brought back the moaning of the Atlantic in the long sleepless nights, while she thought of what her life was to be as the mother of a nameless child. Love had died the death between the night of agonised farewell and these hours of weary waiting. And when her aunt, sitting by her bed in the deep of night—when she felt in her utter weakness as if she were drifting upon a sluggish river, drifting to darkness and ease—told her very gently that her child was dead, and that her secret and her shame had died with him, she had neither the sorrow of a woman with the maternal instinct, nor the thankfulness of a worldling.

She thought and hoped that she too would soon be dead, and that she had come to the last link in the chain of misery. Had he not made her suffer, this man, who wrote so glibly, and offered her the delight of revisiting the scenes fraught with such bitter memories? What of happiness had she ever known from the night they parted, till she met Conrad Harling, and knew the meaning of a good man's love? Her dearest, her truest, most generous, most chivalrous of men, in whose large heart no taint of self-love had ever entered!

And was she to surrender that noble lover, to give herself to the man whose sensual passion had blighted her life, the unscrupulous seducer, who could not respect the innocence of a girl just escaped from a school where evil things were unknown, where every book and every lesson, every allusion to the outer world, was chosen with a studious reverence for youthful purity.

This man must be answered. She knew how impatient, how persistent he could be, how in that brief time when she had begun to fear him, with some instinctive prescience of her danger, he had pursued every advantage, seized upon every opportunity of that unconventional life, how he had hunted and waylaid her. He would have to be answered, and at once.

She was long writing that answer, though her letter was brief.

The church clocks struck two before she had addressed and sealed it.

"The past is past," she began. "It was more dreadful to me than you can ever know. I have only one favour to ask. Forget me, as I have tried to forget you. I am going to marry a man whom I dearly love, and I know that you are too honourable, and I hope you are too kind, to come between me and that great happiness. Let the dead bury their dead. I have never reproached you. I have never breathed your name to anyone belonging to me. No one knows how cruel you were to a helpless girl. No one will ever know from my lips. Perhaps you think it would be a kind of reparation if you were to marry me; but believe me there is only one reparation in your power, and that is to be a stranger to me for the rest of our lives."

There was no signature. Her penmanship would be sufficient evidence against her should he be wicked enough to show her letter to anyone who knew her; but that was a depth of infamy of which she could not suppose him capable. Reparation! That was what his letter meant. Their marriage was to make everything happy; and that miserable past was to be thought of as a fairy tale of girlish love, a memory of days that had been sweet, to be dwelt upon in sentimental moments amidst the security of married life.

This was the man she ought to marry, this man whose coarse mind could conceive no shame in the remembrance of sin. She was bound to him by that shameful past. He had the right to claim her. He was the only man upon earth to whom she could go as a bride without dishonour.

She could realise this stern truth, and yet reject his offer, resolved to give herself only to the man she loved: her *preux chevalier*, her Phœbus Apollo, radiant in the glory of enchanting youth, frank, joyous, a creature made for happiness, made to be adored. She had discovered a likeness in Conrad's clear-cut Greek features to the Belvedere Apollo. He had the same outlook, his head had the same poise. And he loved her with a passion as pure as it was strong, loved her with the love that sees something of divinity in the chosen wife.

It was four o'clock before she fell asleep, and then sleep was worse than waking, for Henry Middlemore's image was mixed with the trouble of her dreams.

When the maid brought the morning tea she sent her to Lady Thelliston to say that she had a bad headache and would not leave her room till after church-time.

She would get up at about eleven o'clock, she told the maid, and would want no help in dressing after her clothes were put out; the white crêpe frock, the pansy toque, and so forth. If Mr. Harling called, he was to be told she would be in the drawing-room at a quarter to one ready to go for a walk. And then she drank her tea, and lay down again, trying to compose herself, trying to bring the colour back to her pallid cheeks, the brightness to her haggard eyes. She badly wanted to sleep, she longed to sink into the gulf of oblivion, the darkness where memory and pain are not.

That deep oblivion would not come at her bidding, only fitful snatches of slumber, with intervals of restlessness, fretful movements, rebellion against fate. Had she not suffered enough? Had she not a right to be happy after those quenching fires, that heavy price paid for sin? Duty! Truth! Honour! Those were mere words when weighed in the balance against happiness and love. She knew that, if she kept her secret, she could make Conrad happy. She knew that to tell him the story of her fall would be to make him miserable, perhaps to plunge him again into the darkness of that living death of the lunatic asylum, he whose exuberant nature was made for the glory of life, made to be happy and to diffuse gladness.

Conrad's card was lying on the hall-table when she went downstairs at twelve o'clock, and crept out of the house to post her letter. A messenger was of course impossible. The man must wait till Monday morning for her answer.

He would be angry no doubt, surprised and indignant at her refusal, but she did not think he would try to injure her.

There was a pillar-post a few doors off, and her absence had lasted less than five minutes. The footman looked surprised when he opened the door for her, no one having heard her go out.

"Mr. Harling called at nine o'clock to inquire for you, ma'am. Brixham gave him your message, and he said he would be here soon after twelve."

She had only been just in time with her letter. Conrad appeared before she had been in the drawing-room five minutes, enchanted to find her waiting for him, ready for their Sunday-morning walk, full of solicitude about her health, needing to be assured that she had quite recovered from the headache that his folly had caused.

They went to Hamilton Gardens, Conrad rejoicing in the little bit of solitude they might have before people came out of church, Irene's share of the conversation being performed very feebly. She had seen Henry Middlemore on the other side of the way as they crossed Hill Street, and she thought that he might be going to the house to make some inquiry about her, after being disappointed of a letter in the morning. Oh, the horror of it all, if he were going to dog her footsteps, to haunt her, to hunt her down! She had tried to believe it was impossible that he should persecute her, that he must have some generous feeling, some touch of remorse that would induce him to spare her, when once he realised that her love was dead, that another and a better love had come into its place. He knew nothing yet, and no doubt was acting upon the presumption that she still loved him, and would forgive everything for love's sake.

And then there was something else that he did not know; the slow fire of shame, the shame that had burnt into her heart and brain, and had killed love.

She was glad when the gate closed behind them, and they were walking in the exclusive Eden, where the few could escape from the many.

"I want to talk of something very serious," Conrad said, and seeing her sudden, scared look: "My dearest, don't be frightened. It isn't anything gloomy or horrid. I want you to fix our wedding day. We are always talking about it as coming soon, and I know your frocks are being made, but we have been vague so far. Let it be soon, love, very soon!"

They were alone in the shelter of the trees, and he could even venture to slip his arm through hers, and draw her a little nearer to him, his ear on the alert for approaching footsteps.

"When shall it be, love?"

"You must settle that with my step-mother. I'm afraid she'll want to make a fuss and invite people—my father's friends—most of them soldiers. Let it be as soon as she likes. I want to belong to you, Conrad. I want to be sure that we are bound to each other for life."

He was enraptured at her speech, the most direct avowal of love he had ever had from her.

"My sweet girl, you have filled my cup of bliss. I'll talk to Lady Thelliston after lunch. She can order the invitation cards to-morrow morning. They ought to be ready in twenty-four hours; and a fortnight's invitation will be enough."

"Wedding invitations are generally much longer."

"That's only to give people time to buy presents. We don't want candlesticks or paper-knives, do we?"

"What can I want? You have loaded me with lovely things."

"Nothing half lovely enough. The jewellers have no new ideas. They can only offer one something that they made last week for a duchess or a countess. They have no new departures. One must go to Italy for an idea."

They walked in the gardens till half-past one, no longer in bliss-ful solitude, but meeting people they knew every five minutes. They were on the way back to Chapel Street, when in the little street by Dorchester House they came into a group of people, and stopped to talk, and while Conrad was monopolised by a loqua-cious dowager, Irene found Henry Middlemore at her side. She had not seen him coming, did not know where he had sprung from.

"I hope you haven't forgotten me, Miss Thelliston," he said, offering his hand, and then he went on in a much lower voice: "No letter! If you knew how I am devoured by impatience!"

"I posted my answer an hour ago."

"Cruel! I shan't get it till to-morrow. An eternity!"

People were talking all round her, yet she was in an agony lest Conrad should hear. She broke in upon the dowager's discourse.

"We shall be very late for luncheon," she said.

Middlemore lifted his hat and went away, but those few words, his persistence in talking to her when she was among people, had given her an agony of fear. The chattering group dispersed.

"There was no escape from that woman," Conrad said. "That was the man we met yesterday, wasn't it? The man whose horse won?"

"Yes."

"What a presuming cad to talk to you."

She did not answer him. She walked by his side in dull silence. Middlemore's persistence filled her with dread. He had waited for her while she was in the gardens, watched and followed her when she came out. Despair came upon her suddenly as she realised her peril. A word, a look, from this man might awaken Conrad's suspicions. He would question her, drive her to distraction, force her to prevaricate and to lie; and doubt once awakened, the fierce suspicion of jealous love, he would not rest till he had dragged her secret from her, would not be appeased till the veil was rent from that disgraceful story, and he knew her for the thing she was.

And then to be thrown off and abandoned, to see the warm fond lover turned into a man of stone, cruel to himself as to her, inflexible even in his despair. She had learnt to know his way of thinking, all his opinions, prejudices, beliefs; and she knew that an unvirtuous woman was hateful in his eyes. She had watched his countenance when improper people had been discussed in his presence, lightly, with a smoothing over of hard facts, and she knew that in his mind there was no indulgence for sin. His chivalrous ideas about women were allied with a severity as of the seventeenth century Puritans.

She hardly knew how she lived through the rest of the day. She dined at home, and went with Lady Thelliston to a rather prim evening-party where she was to meet Conrad and his mother. She tried to avoid Lady Mary, feeling that those keen clear eyes would read her trouble, might even divine the cause, and know that her first lover had come back into her life.

She heard two men talking of him as the owner of yesterday's winner.

"Not half a bad fellow—very popular in his own part of the country—an invalid wife—died at Cannes last winter. They want him to take the hounds next season—plenty of money."

And then the conversation changed and she heard no more of him.

It was a dull party, though there were three or four well-known politicians and more than one artistic and literary celebrity in the little crowd. There was no music, and by a quarter-past eleven everybody had gone on, or had gone home. Conrad had hardly left Irene's side, and she had tried to talk lightly and to seem gay. He told her of his satisfactory conversation with her step-mother. The wedding invitations were to be ordered next morning, and sent out on Wednesday—a ten days' invitation.

"And now you have only to make up your mind about the honeymoon. Where shall we go? To what secluded nook in Switzerland—or on the Italian side of Montblanc, and then down into Italy, to Locano, Baveno, Stresa. To be together and alone in that divine country! Think what bliss!"

All this was spoken in confidential tones while they sat under an awning on the balcony in a thicket of palms.

He was radiant with the assurance of happiness, expectant of a life without a cloud. He asked about the bridesmaids. Had she chosen them, and how many? Daisy, of course, must be one of them.

"My step-mother insisted upon six bridesmaids—girls whose mothers were her bridesmaids. She knows crowds of people. I know she has asked your cousin, and Miss Meredith has kindly consented to be one of the six. My father and I would have liked a quiet wedding—just one bridesmaid—but I suppose Lady Mary would think that kind of thing rather discreditable."

"Oh, I daresay she will approve of Lady Thelliston's plans. She will like a little fuss. But if I could marry you to-morrow morning in the quietest church in London—some dear old City church—St. Andrew's, Holborn, for instance, and whisk you off to Lucerne in the Engadine Express, I should think myself the most blessed of men."

She sat by his side in silence, with a heart of ice, remembering how that other man had pleaded for a quiet wedding, and a swift flight to fairer scenes, to that unutterably beautiful world, the valley girt round with snow-mountains where they had met and loved and parted.

She let her hand lie in Conrad's, and he bent down and kissed it in the shadow of the palms. The beautiful head with the short crisp brown hair bent down to worship her, and while he worshipped there was another man claiming her as if by an indefeasible right.

She rode in the Park with her father and Conrad next morning, rejoicing in her Arab's freshness and the gallop that brought the colour back to her cheeks. Between Stanhope Gate and the Row she had time to think what an escape it would be if she could bring about an accident, make her horse bolt with her and break his neck and hers over the railings. She remembered a favourite novel in which she had read of such a catastrophe, and how in the story sudden death had solved a problem, as it might solve the problem of her life. If she were killed that morning Conrad would never know.

His mother would not break her oath. Lady Mary would be content to know that he was released from the bond she hated; and Death would cancel Henry Middlemore's claim.

Conrad reproached her for riding wildly.

"If you ride with such a loose rein I shall be afraid to let you ride to hounds," he said.

He had talked to her of the hunting next year, and that he might take the hounds perhaps, by and by. They were to winter in Egypt; but there might be a chance of some good sport in March, when they went home.

Home! The word had been sweet in her ears; but now there was the blackness of impenetrable night round her, dread, and almost despair.

There was a letter lying on the hall-table when she went in, exactly like the last, a conspicuous letter with a big vermilion seal, delivered by hand.

"Who's your correspondent?" her father asked sharply, as she took up the letter.

"Oh, it's nothing of importance."

"Is it a bill?"

"No; only a circular."

She ran upstairs before he could ask any more questions, and shut herself in her room.

Her frock was laid out on the bed, and Justine would be engaged with Lady Thelliston for the next two hours. She was safe in her seclusion till eleven o'clock, when Daisy was to call for her, and they were to go together to the people who were making her trousseau, and who had to be kept up to time.

This was the letter she had to read, she who ardently desired to know herself bound to Conrad Harling through life and till death. Within less than a fortnight of the day appointed for her wedding she had to read this letter and consider all that it meant:

"Your letter, just to hand, is a thunderbolt. I suppose I had no right to expect that you would remain free; and indeed when we parted, when I left you with an aching heart to fulfil an engagement from which I saw no escape, I told myself that I hoped you would meet with someone better worthy of your love, that you would make a happy marriage, and that all we had been to each other would seem to you no more than the memory of a dream. Could I think otherwise in that dark day when I was leaving you, as I thought, for ever, to keep faith with the woman to whom I had bound myself before I had ever seen your love-compelling face.

"But now that there is no barrier to our happiness, now that the one desire of my heart and mind is to call you wife, it seems to me impossible that any other man can stand between us. Remember what you have been to me, and ask yourself if you can refuse to be mine, now that Providence has put it in our power to cancel all that was unfortunate in the past by the most solemn, the most sacred of bonds. Can you for an instant contemplate giving yourself to another man while I am here to remind you of my claim, I who am the only man living who has any right over you? What power of choice can you have in such circumstances? Can I believe that you will call another man husband and deny yourself to me, whose overmastering passion brought shipwreck upon us both, when you were a child in ignorance of evil, a woman only in the power to love.

"Oh, my divine girl, think of those days, think of all we were to each other, my Haidee, so lovely and so innocent. I was a wretch to hazard the sweet enchantment of those hours, a wretch not to fly temptation, not to leave you while you could still remember me without pain. But if I made you unhappy then I can give you a life of devotion in atonement for my sin. Do not try to cheat me. Do not imagine that I will forego my right to make you my wife, without needless delay. In the face of your letter, I shall not rest till you are legally mine. I shall apply for the special license to-day, and shall leave this hotel and take rooms in your parish.

"Yours and yours only till death us do part,

"H. M."

All the more determined phrases were heavily underscored. From the first words to the last the letter was a menace. She remembered the tyranny of his love in the days when she had loved him. She was then at the age when a girl adores a tyrant. His determined pursuit of her had been the charm that worked to such fatal issues. To be pursued, to be worshipped! It was the school-girl's dream of bliss. But now, with this letter in her hand, remembering what he had been, a deadly fear took hold of her. He had been her master then, when she loved him. He was her master now, when she hated him. How could she have hoped that he would be generous, that he would stand out of her way and let her take her own road to happiness?

How could she have hoped that pity, or honour would seal his lips, when he wanted to marry her? Self was his god and his law. She knew that now, recalling details remembered though not understood in those foolish hours, before she had acquired wisdom in the school of misery.

He would have no mercy.

What could she do? She dared not defy him. She had told him that love was dead, and he had ignored that plea. He wanted her. He would make her his bond slave, and would laugh at the power of a rival. He would make her marry him. There was the sickening dread that froze her. She saw herself at his mercy. If she persisted in refusing him he would fight for her with the most odious weapons, would tell her lover all that cruellest speech could tell of her sin-stained girlhood. She would stand before her *preux chevalier*, the man who worshipped her, a lost creature.

She had told Lady Mary that Conrad would cleave to her, even if he heard her story. The disillusion might go near to break his heart, but he would not forsake her. He would take her, degraded, humiliated, changed utterly from the goddess he had worshipped, and would pardon and pity her. But love and life would be changed; and she told herself that she could not live under the burden of his pity, she could not live with him and be happy, conscious of the change in his feelings. Better—better anything—than to be *his* wife, knowing that she had forfeited his respect, that he was sorry for her, and sorry for himself as her husband.

What was she to do? She had no hour in the day that she could call her own, no power to go the length of Chapel Street without accounting for her moments. Her step-mother was too self-absorbed to be formidable; but she had an idea that her father suspected her, that those cold cruel eyes followed and watched her. He had looked at her keenly when he questioned her about that dreadful letter—so obviously *not* a tradesman's circular.

She was like a hunted stag at bay, the cry of the pack gaining on her. She had no time to think, no time to map out her course. An imperative message had come from her father before she had taken off her riding clothes; he was at breakfast and wanted to see her. It was her daily task to pour out his coffee, and to pretend they were on excellent terms, a model father and daughter. He was a man who loved shams.

At eleven Daisy came for her in Lady Mary's victoria, and she was driven to Dover Street to spend a weary hour trying on garments of every description—her wedding dress—her clothes for Italy—and her clothes for Egypt. Conrad was pacing the street, waiting for them to come out and join him, and then they were to go and walk in the Park by the sumptuous flowerbeds, while the driving people and the riding people and the walking people went by them like figures in a cinematograph. To Irene on that miserable day nothing in the world seemed real except her own despair. A few yards from Stanhope Gate she saw Henry Middlemore standing with his back to the railings watching them. She looked straight before her, and went on talking to Daisy, pretending not to see him.

"That man haunts us," Conrad said, when they had passed.

"What man?"

"The owner of Horoscope. Didn't you see him?"

"No."

She managed to post a letter to Middlemore that afternoon—hiding it between other letters and dropping it into a pillar box before Conrad's eyes, as they walked through Esher, where the Mercedes had carried them to take tea in an inn garden, Daisy and Professor Wilmer for their companions, the Professor attaching himself to Daisy in a dull persistent way, like a learned barnacle. He was never weary of expounding his views about the universe for her edification, and he had told her incidentally that he would like to marry her.

Conrad was to dine in Chapel Street, and to meet his betrothed at two dances.

Her letter to Middlemore was brief:

"If you will walk in the Park, by the flowerbeds, between Stanhope and Grosvenor Gate, to-morrow morning at half-past six, I will try to join you for a quarter of an hour. There is no use in any more letter-writing."

That was all; no signature, no address.

Such an appointment was a desperate thing; but she thought it would be safe at that early hour. No servant would come downstairs before seven, and she would only have to unbolt the street door and go out. Her father came down at eight for his morning ride. She could be back at the house at a quarter-past seven, in time to put on her habit. The servants could do no more than wonder. They might think she had gone out for an early walk with her fiancé.

The second and more delightful of the two dances did not begin to languish till after three o'clock, when Lady Thelliston declared herself absolutely worn out, a fact confirmed by the damaged state of her complexion, and insisted on carrying off her step-daughter, in spite of Conrad's petition for one more "extra." Irene had been paramount in beauty, crowned with the factitious interest of approaching nuptials, all other girls curious about her, and most of them inclined to depreciate her charms, and to consider Mr. Harling much too good for her.

"No doubt she was very pretty, in a certain style of her own—rather like Lady Hamilton in Romney's pictures;* and, well, everybody knew what kind of person his famous sitter was. Quite a Romney beauty! And she had dropped from the skies last June. She had no connexions about the Court. The King had asked who she was in a tone that implied a great deal. She had not even been presented on this side of the Irish Channel. She was going to be after her marriage. The father was a soldier, but no one had heard of him till that West African affair the other day. The mother—or step-mother—was too odious for words. In point of fact, they had no connexions whatever, that anybody knew of. They were quite new people, and they were living in a squeezy little house in Chapel Street, quite impossible for entertaining."

In such phrases did the faded and the partnerless express their poor opinion of Irene and her people.

The sky was sunless and grey, and there was a chilliness in the air when Irene stole out of the house soon after six o'clock to keep her appointment with Middlemore. Her endeavour to sleep in the daylight and amidst the sound of awakening birds and early traffic had been vain. Two and a half hours of restlessness had made her more tired than when she left the dance, and she had that strange vague feeling of not being more than half alive which comes from sleepless nights and the strain of hidden trouble. From Saturday afternoon till Tuesday morning her brain had been working at an eighty-horse power, not an hour's natural sleep, not a minute's respite from torturing thoughts in her waking hours, not even when she was waltzing with her lover in the flower-scented ballroom, gliding round in an elysium of music and light, his strong arm encircling her, his kind eyes watching her face with ineffable love. No, there had been no pause in the torment of the labouring brain. What was she to do? Was there any hope, any way of escape from the doom she loathed: to part from the man she loved, to give herself to the man she hated?

Now in the chill grey morning, past the awakening flowers, she was hurrying to meet the hated lover, to fight her last battle for freedom, and make her last appeal to the tyrant. The cool air revived her, and that dream-like feeling of not being quite conscious of existence, which amounted almost to the loss of identity, left her in the freshness of the morning.

It was not a quarter past six when she went into the Park, but Middlemore was there before her, a few yards from Grosvenor Gate. She saw the tall figure, broad and stalwart, coming towards her with a swinging step, on the solitary path. There was no one else within sight. They had the Park to themselves.

He almost ran to meet her, and before she could speak he was holding her in his arms, and his kisses were on her face, the kisses of love that will not be denied. She gave a cry of despair, and struggled to escape, but the strong arms held her close. She felt like some wild thing that had fallen into a trap.

"My angel, how sweet of you to come," he said, with his lips on her face.

She went on struggling impotently. Her cheeks, that had been white when she met him, were flaming with angry fire.

"Let me go," she gasped. "You don't know how I hate you."

"No, no, if you hated me you would not have come. No, no, it is love that brings my Haidee to my arms."

He saw people coming—a sauntering policeman—a groom exercising a horse, and released her from that fierce embrace, and slipped his arm through hers, and led her across the road to the turf under the trees, where they might walk unseen. She was trembling violently, and the weakness of strained nerves made her helpless.

"Let me sit down, or I shall faint," she said, and he took her to a bench and seated her by his side, with his arm round her. He took off her hat and made her rest her head against his shoulder, and held her as a man holds a woman who is his own. There was a rough tenderness in all he did, a tenderness that had been enchanting in the old days, when the glamour of unknown love held her spell-bound and at his mercy.

"I came to you to tell you that I mean to marry Conrad Harling," she said, when she could command her voice.

"Not while I live—not while I live. You are my wife in the sight of God. You must wait till you are my widow if you want to marry any other man."

"No, I am not your wife. I owe you nothing. You have not the shadow of a right over me. You left me to my misery, to my shame."

She burst into tears, and hid her face in her hands, sobbing violently. The loosely rolled-up hair fell over her neck and shoulders. Middlemore sat for a minute in deep thought; then with extreme tenderness, with hands that caressed the lovely tresses, he bound them into a knot and gathered up the scattered combs and made her head look neat again.

"You spoke of shame," he said in a low voice. "What shame could there be—except in my sweet girl's tender conscience?"

"There was shame—bitter shame—a year of shame. It was a year after you forsook me—before I could go into the light of day without shrinking from every eye—hating my fellow-creatures—a year before I left my sick bed—a wreck! Ah, if you had seen me then you would not have wanted me. Such a wasted sickly creature would have no attraction for you."

He hardly heard what she said. He took her to his breast again with irresistible force.

"My beloved girl—I never dreamt—I never for a moment contemplated—— Oh, what a brute I was! But you told me nothing—you never hinted at your trouble. How could I think that you would have kept such a secret? Our child! Oh, how I shall adore—how I shall worship my Haidee's child—son or daughter! How divine a gift! Where—where have you hidden our child?"

"In the grave," she answered. "He did not live through the day."

"My angel! My suffering angel! But we have life before us; and we are going to be happy. And could you think of marrying another man—you, the mother of my son? It was a shameful thought."

There was a change in his accent, as he spoke those words, a change to absolute severity.

"It was a shameful thought."

That was this man's opinion; and how about the other man whom she adored—her *preux chevalier*? If she could defy Middlemore and marry Conrad Harling, might not the day come when he would tell her that it was a shameful thought, a shameful act that had given her to his arms? Would love excuse her? Would beauty win his pardon, beauty disfigured by sin?

No, she could not marry Conrad. She could not face the possibility of his anger, his grief, his killing contempt.

Perhaps she had known from the moment when Henry Middlemore took her in his arms that the battle was lost.

She had come into the cool grey morning, braced with angry resolution, prepared to fight a desperate battle, determined to win. But he had given her no chance of fighting. She was his prey. He had taken possession of her. He had held it unquestionable that she must be his. The old tyranny subjugated her, something there might be perhaps of the old magnetism, when the lightest touch of that strong hand, trembling as it stirred the lilies upon her breast, had thrilled her with girlhood's unquestioning love.

She knew that the battle was lost. After her passion of sobs she sat looking straight before her, with tearless eyes, conquered—despairing.

"I suppose you would be sorry if I were to kill myself," she said at last, in a low toneless voice.

"No, no; you will not kill yourself. You bore that year of martyrdom, my poor dove. Why should you want to die now when you have a happy life before you? You think you are in love with this Harling fellow, but that's skittles! He is younger than I am, altogether more attractive, I daresay; but I am the man you loved when first your heart knew what love meant. I am the man you will love till your dying day."

She made no fight. She sat mute and defeated, and let him dictate to her.

"We can be married at nine o'clock to-morrow morning. You have only to slip out of your house at half-past eight. I shall be in the street watching for you. Don't trouble about bag or baggage. I will get all you can want for a few weeks—and after that no doubt your people will send your things. They may make a fuss at first;

but when they find you have married a man of good means they'll come round like a shot."

A clock struck seven.

"I must go home," she said, putting on her hat.

She did not look at him, or answer him. She neither assented nor refused. She made no protest, except for a long agonised sigh. She was beaten.

He walked with her till they were within sight of the flowery balconies, holding her arm all the way. She felt his love sustaining her, dominating her as in the past. She knew that it was real love of its kind; violent, tyrannical, exacting, but real. She knew that he was ready to fight for her, to do wild and desperate things rather than let her go.

A housemaid opened the door and stared at her in blank surprise.

"I have been walking in the Park to cure my headache," she explained. "Tell Clarkson to let the groom know that my horse won't be wanted, and he can tell Sir Michael that I am not going to ride this morning."

She flung herself upon the bed, beaten, beaten! She felt as if the beating had been not only moral but physical. Heart and limbs were aching. She wanted to lie upon the ground, face downwards, and never get up again. Middlemore had trodden her into the dust.

She did not leave her room that day. She refused to see Conrad. She sent him a line in pencil to tell him she was tired to death after the ball, and must take a day's rest. He rushed off to an eminent nerve-doctor who lived within a stone's-throw, and gave himself no peace till that authority had seen the beloved patient, and could assure him that there was nothing seriously amiss, only nervous prostration, requiring seclusion and repose. An affair of a day or two.

That was all; but for Conrad the world was empty. He hardly knew how to get through the day. His only relief was in talking to Daisy about the wedding—asking trivial questions about the frocks, about the bridesmaids, about the bride's luggage.

"Shall we go and look at her trunks?" he asked, as if proposing a treat, and he straightway carried the submissive Daisy to the trunk-makers, where he gloated over the great dress-box, the hat-boxes and bags, the cabin trunk for the voyage to Alexandria. They were to be finished off in a hurry, with her initials I. H., and a four-leaved shamrock by way of badge on sides and lid.

"Lady Thelliston is to find her a good maid," said Conrad. "The poor darling has had only a half share in her step-mother's slavey up to now."

"Judging by Lady Thelliston's complexion it would be more like a sixteenth," said Daisy.

Conrad rode with the General next morning. Irene was under the doctor's orders to keep her room.

"She has been doing too much," Sir Michael said. "Girls are simply insatiable. My poor wife is worn out. I heard them come in on Monday night, I should say Tuesday morning, a few minutes to four."

Conrad talked of Irene all the time. Would Sir Michael send her Arab to Cranford, where the stud groom would take particular care of him, in a loose box, with his shoes off, till the spring, when they came home from Egypt. She should have her Arabs there, and revel in the desert rides, the delicious mornings, the charm and wonder of that land of strange gods.

"Curious to think how we humdrum English have taken possession of it after all these centuries," he said, "and how we carry all our paltry modern luxuries, our fine clothes and snobbism, to the land that was old when Herodotus wrote about it."

He breakfasted with his mother and Daisy. He was restless and yet dull, as if that severance of twenty-four hours had been too much for his nerves. Lady Mary watched him anxiously. She felt as if there were thunder in the air. She had noted the change in Irene's manner on Sunday. And now the girl's nervous breakdown puzzled her, while the hurrying on of the wedding was a blow. It killed the remnant of hope, that slowly dwindling hope she had cherished from the beginning of Conrad's engagement, the hope that something would happen, and that her son would be saved from that unholy union.

She had submitted to the inevitable. She had been tolerant, and had put on a show of kindness in her intercourse with Irene; but the memory of that night on board the *Electra*, the shock of the girl's confession, had never been out of her mind since the hour she knew this girl was to be her son's wife.

Conrad had called in Chapel Street before breakfast, carrying a tribute of hot-house flowers for Irene, with an eight-page letter written after midnight. He told his mother of this visit while they were at breakfast.

"She won't leave her room till the doctor has seen her," he said; "but I know she'd like to see you, Daisy, if you will go and look her up."

"And you want me to tell you how she looks, and what she says. If she is quite a wreck after being a day under the weather; if she has cried herself blind at being parted from you," Daisy said, laughing at him, full of kindness, resigned to the certainty that he was to pass out of *her* life altogether in a few days.

"Tell her I shall call before lunch to hear what the doctor has said, and if I may take her into the country in the afternoon. We might go to Brighton, and give her a breath of sea air, and be back by nine o'clock for dinner."

He went off to his den at the back of the house, carrying the *Times* with him, and totally incapable of reading it.

They had sat at breakfast longer than usual, and it was ten o'clock when Lady Mary went to her morning-room.

"You can go to Chapel Street before you come for my letters," she told Daisy. "There is nothing very important this morning," whereupon Daisy went off meekly to put on her hat and to go and worship at the shrine of the strange goddess.

She passed the Thellistons' footman on the way, walking towards Hertford Street, and the butler who opened the door had a certain discomposure in his looks.

Miss Thelliston was not at home.

"Then she is better, I hope," said Daisy, "if she has really gone out."

"Yes," the man assured her. Miss Thelliston had gone out early, a few minutes after Sir Michael started for his ride.

Daisy retraced her steps, wondering greatly.

Conrad came out of his den and met her in the hall.

"Back already? They would not let you see her?" he asked excitedly.

"She was not at home."

"Not at home? Nonsense!"

"The butler said so."

He snatched up his hat, and hurried out of the house.

A letter had been taken to Lady Mary five minutes before—a letter carried by the footman Daisy had met on her way to Chapel Street.

"Tuesday night.

"You have won, Lady Mary. I am beaten in my battle for life and love; but not by you.

"Fate has been too cruel. The man you know of has come back to me, free to make me his wife, and he has compelled me to marry him.

"There is no help for me. I have fought hard, but he has conquered me. We are to be married early to-morrow morning. We are to leave England to-morrow night. I go to him with a broken heart. I can never love him, never respect him, never hope for happiness with him, remembering what Conrad has been to me, my noble lover, my king of men. Ah, you can never know how I have loved your son, or how happy I could have made him, with an adoring wife's devotion, obedience, unchanging fidelity, if fate had let me.

"I have had to succumb. If I were to persist in refusing Henry Middlemore, some dreadful thing would happen. It is best that I should be the sacrifice. I deserve nothing better.

"I thought that he had gone out of my life for ever, that he was no more to me than the memory of a bad dream. But I met him at Sandown on Saturday, and from that hour I have had no peace.

"You tried to shame me into giving up your son, and you failed. Henry Middlemore has shamed me into marrying him; and your son has escaped.

"Will you break this news to him, and be merciful to me, and keep the secret which you swore never to betray, on your crucifix? I do not think you could ever look upon that sacred image without dread if you were to break that oath. Never let him know of that dark stain upon my life. Never let him know that he has been twice the dupe of a pretty face. But, indeed, I hope at my worst I am better than the Innkeeper's daughter, for, at least, I have loved him fondly and disinterestedly, and I would have married him had he been a beggar, and would have been proud to call him husband.

"Have pity upon me now, Lady Mary, as you had that night on the *Electra*, for I am in as deep a pit of shame and sorrow.

"IRENE THELLISTON."

Lady Mary sat staring into vacancy, with the girl's open letter on the table before her. He had escaped. The union she had dreaded and loathed, the union of honour with dishonour, was not to be. He had escaped this danger; but could she dare to be glad, while that other and even worse peril threatened him? The peril of a mind overthrown by a sudden, overwhelming grief.

She knew how he loved this girl. She had seen the self-surrender, the total absorption of his whole being, in that young love. She knew that from the night of the ball, from the hour when he had held the lovely girl in his arms, from their first waltz, from their first interchange of trivial talk, sitting among the palms and flowers in the half light of a winter garden, he had existed only to adore her. Irene had become his world, and there was nothing else worth living for. Restless, silent, pre-occupied in her absence, he woke to radiant life when she appeared. The light stereotyped amusements of each day had become Elysian joys. Only to be with her had made the dull earth fairyland.

And now he was to be told that his goddess had been stolen from him—that the creature who was so soon to have been his own, his own for life, had been taken from him for ever.

Would it mend matters to tell him that she was worthless, that to marry her would have been a calamity? No; the revelation would only give a sharper edge to his grief, the agony of knowing that he had been fooled for the second time in his life.

He burst into the room while Lady Mary sat looking at the tree-tops and the blue summer sky with unseeing eyes.

"Mother, a letter has been brought to you—Irene's letter. What does it mean? She is gone—no one knows where! It's maddening! Give me her letter."

He would have snatched the open letter from under his mother's hand, but she spread her hand over it, holding it on the table.

"No, no; you are not to read her letter."

A despatch-box stood open on the table in front of her. She threw the letter into it and put down the lid, which fastened with a spring lock. Then turning to her son, she put her arms round his neck and drew his face down against her own.

"My dearest son, be brave! Try to bear the heaviest blow you have ever had. If you could know how I love you, how my life is bound up in you, I think you would be brave for my sake."

"Where has she gone? Why? Why?"

He was white to the lips, and his voice was hoarse and dull. And then, to his mother's horror, he burst suddenly into a laugh.

"She was like the publican's daughter, I suppose. There is some-one she liked better—some great coarse brute who knew how to master her."

He remembered the man at Sandown, the man who had talked to Irene at the corner of Stanhope Street on Sunday—the man he had seen leaning against the Park rails on Monday morning.

"She has gone off with that fellow? That's what's the matter. Can't you speak?" he cried furiously.

"She was married early this morning—to Mr. Middlemore. It is not a happy marriage, Conrad. You have more reason to pity her than to blame her."

"Pity her, yes, I must pity her, pity her for breaking my heart, for making me hate the world I live in—and all human kind—except you. I'll make that one exception, mother, though you did me the biggest wrong you could do when you brought me into this vile world. This world of lovely faces and black hearts. Black, black as Erebus.* Oh, how I loved her! How I trusted in her love! And she was to make me happy! That was the burden of her song: 'I mean to make you happy.' And she let me fix our wedding-day—last Sunday. She melted into my arms, and sighed, and said it could not be too soon. At that moment she was as utterly mine as wedded wife ever was. Mine by the beating of her heart, by the lips that trembled as I kissed them. And she has married that coarse brute—a creature of thews and sinews, a face flushed with high living. Do you say that they are married—now, now, as we stand here?"

"They were married early this morning, and they are to leave England to-night. Conrad, my idolised son, only tell me that you will show yourself a strong man—strong in moral force——"

"You mean that I will grin and bear it—take my licking a little better than I did before. Don't be frightened, mother. I am not going back to Roehampton. She has killed the gladness of my life; but I won't let her kill mind and memory—if I can help it. I won't bring trouble upon you again—if I can help it."

He went out of the room after these words and Lady Mary did not follow him. She must let him fight his own battle. He had taken the blow a little better than she had hoped, but his ghastly pallor and the strained look in his eyes had appalled her. The warning of the doctors was ever present in her mind.

"Don't let him be disappointed a second time."

The disappointment had come, by no act of hers; and he had to bear the blow, and live through the agony of it as best he could. She knew that she could do nothing to help him. The maternal heart might ache for him, but a mother's affection could not heal the wounds a fatal love had made. All attempts at consolation would be but a repetition of phrases that would fall upon the sensitive brain like the measured water-drops in the torture chamber.

CHAPTER IX

CONRAD went straight to Chapel Street, where he found Sir Michael Thelliston in the den behind the dining-room, a place where he kept his boots and the scanty literature of the establishment.

"Oh, my dear Harling, I was just going to Hertford Street—my dear, dear fellow!"

"I suppose you know why she has done this thing?"

"My dear fellow, I know no more—hardly anything more—than you do yourself."

"Oh, but you must. She must have been in love with this man. She would not jilt me a fortnight before our wedding-day if there were not some kind of tie between her and this man. She must have been in love with him when they met in Cashmere—and then they lost sight of each other, I suppose; and last Saturday he came back into her life, and whistled, as he would have whistled for his dog—and she went after him."

"She may have cared for him, perhaps—in Cashmere. I was not there with her. My niece told me that Irene was greatly admired. She was not eighteen, just out of the schoolroom; but my niece said she was turning heads; and this—this Middlemore was among her admirers."

"Is that all you can tell me?"

"Yes, that's about all."

"And her step-mother, does she know no more than this?"

"She knows nothing. She is horribly upset, as I am. I was proud of my girl's engagement to you, proud of such a son-in-law. It is a diabolical stroke of fate. I know nothing of this man; he may be the biggest brute in England."

"Did she write to you?"

"Only a line to say that she was to be married this morning at nine o'clock, at St. Nectern's, to Henry Middlemore. The letter was brought by a messenger, after ten o'clock. I went round to the church, but the doors were shut."

"Well, she has made her choice. I thought she loved me; but it seems I am easily deceived. God knows I loved her. Good-bye, Sir Michael. You have always been kind to me; but you can understand that I shan't care to see anyone belonging to her."

"No, no; I can easily understand. You have been cruelly wronged. I am ashamed of her. I am deeply distressed. There is a box in her room that is to be sent to you. She has packed all your splendid presents in it."

"Damn the presents! Do you think I want to see those again?"

"But they must be restored to you. That is unavoidable."

The General went with him to the hall door, and wrung his hand at parting, and then went sighing back to his den.

"Fool! Fool!" he muttered. "Thirty thousand a year, and a man who was her slave."

He had found Middlemore's name in the red book.

"Henry Middlemore, late Grenadier Guards, D.L., J.P., of Danewood Park, York; Clubs, Reform, Turf."

Conrad went to St. Nectern's, and unearthed a verger, who let him see the marriage register. There was the latest entry, the commonplace statement of a commonplace fact.

"Henry Middlemore, widower.
Irene Thelliston, spinster."

The witnesses were John Jobling, verger, and Sarah Blake, pew-opener.

He went to his club and he sat in the reading-room all day, behind a newspaper, pretending to read. Anything was better than to go back to Hertford Street, where his mother and Daisy would be watching him, and pitying him, and thinking about him all day long.

He telegraphed to Lady Mary from the club early in the afternoon. . . . "Dining at Arthur's—may be late. Don't sit up for me."

And having done this he curled himself up in a big arm-chair, in an obscure corner, and pretended to sleep. Men went in and out without noticing him. He did not even attempt to dine; but he had some tea at seven o'clock, and then walked to the station at Charing Cross to see the last of the girl he was to have married.

If she was to leave England to-night it would be by that train, he thought. He took a ticket for Dover, for the privilege of being on the platform when the train started, and stood amidst the confusion of anxious passengers and harried porters, waiting for the last look, that look which he swore to himself should be the last.

There was the usual crowd for the boat train, and the faces that passed him all seemed to wear the same expression, hurried, eager, and yet with a certain look of pleased anticipation, as if there were something revivifying in the mere fact of leaving one's country. It was always the same look—till he saw her face, and that was different.

Her husband was walking close beside her, holding her arm, hurrying her footsteps, talking to her, flushed, eager, exultant, like a man who has just won some great stake, and who can scarcely contain himself for joy.

She was dressed in black, an alpaca skirt and coat, a black toque, rather shabby clothes that she had worn in Ireland. Conrad had never before seen her in black, and the change was startling.

She was very pale, and she looked years older. Her face was drawn with mental pain and her eyes looked straight before her. Conrad had never seen despair in a face till to-night. He took a step forward unconsciously, with outstretched arms, as if to snatch her from her doom. The sudden movement was unseen in the crowd. A porter opened the door of a compartment labelled "Engaged," and Middlemore lifted his bride into the carriage. A servant came to the door and handed in travelling bag, rug and sticks; and then went with the porter to see the luggage bestowed. "These two boxes for Dover, those three for Paris."

Conrad saw the new boxes, small and neat, which had evidently been bought for the bride. The bride! She who was to have been his bride. Who was to have journeyed with him over that joyous route, over the dancing sea, to lands that were lovely and strange.

He saw the pale, grief-stricken face till the last moment, till the train moved, and she was gone.

Why had she done this thing? What motive could there have

been for such cruel treason, if its only issue was despair? By what spell had this man held her? The mystery of it all was maddening.

He left the station, and walked through the streets like a man in a dream, till he found himself somehow in St. James's Park. It was dark by that time, the thin darkness of summer, and the stars were shining. He walked slowly, lost in thought, in despairing wonder. Why had she done this thing? The face he had seen was not the face of a bride, but the face of a victim. So might Jephthah's daughter* have looked—wantonly sacrificed to a father's irrational vow.

He walked by the Green Park to Hyde Park, and across the sunburnt grass to Kensington Gardens. It was nearly ten o'clock when he found himself at the north-western extremity of the gardens, facing the railings, and watching the traffic in the Bayswater Road, watching with eyes that saw passing wagons and omnibuses, carts and carriages, as strange things, meaningless, a procession of phantoms.

He took hold of the railings with his bare hands, clutching the iron bars with strained fingers, as if to bring himself back to conscious life by that painful contact of sharp-edged iron against sensitive flesh. Since he left the railway station he had been walking in a semiconscious state, as he had walked on that long journey from Abingdon to Padstow; along what dusty roads, uphill and downhill, across what bleak commons or rolling moorland, he had never known. The same loss of conscious identity had come upon him, or if not the same, something that came too near that perilous state. Memory was shaken. He had lost count of time. Where had he been, what had he been doing, since he heard of Irene's marriage? Was it by days, weeks, or months that the interval had to be measured?

"This means Roehampton," he said to himself, frowning. "No, I will not go mad. Once is enough—once, for one false woman— for one lovely wicked face—the face that lures to madness or to death."

He set himself to count the passing vehicles, standing there for a long time, staring into the road, and watching now an omnibus, now a cab, a smart tradesman's cart, a brougham with flashing lamps, and then the rush of a motor, with great flaring eyes like an angry dragon. He looked at them, and studied them deliberately, and named them to himself.

"No, I won't go mad."

He turned on his heel and walked back to Park Lane.

A woman spoke to him in the shadow of the trees.

"Oh, you poor wretch," he cried, giving her a handful of gold, "you never used any man as badly as I have been used," and passed on with quickened pace, so that she could only stand, gazing at his receding figure, murmuring thanks that he could not hear.

His mother came out of her room as he went upstairs.

"What, you sat up for me after all," he exclaimed, "in spite of my wire."

"I could not rest till I knew you were at home."

"My best of mothers, don't worry yourself. I am going to take this business quietly. I am used to it, you see."

He kissed her, and went up to his own room. His quiet voice and manner gave her some slight comfort, but she lay awake all night, with an aching heart, wondering what to-morrow would bring of grief or terror.

Mother and son breakfasted *tête-à-tête*, Daisy having pretended a headache as an excuse for keeping out of their way.

Conrad was perfectly calm, with the settled calmness of a man who is resolved to bear his burden, and who is strong enough to bear it.

"My dear mother, you must not be anxious about me," he said, looking up and surprising Lady Mary's watchful eyes, full of sad solicitude. "I have come to grief for the second time in my life—which seems hard lines considering that I am not thirty—but I am not going to knock under. Indeed, far from knocking under, I am going to make capital out of my misfortune. Those African travels of mine—the Zambesi, Tanganyika—Nyassa. I am going to make that fairy-tale a true story."

"You want to go to Africa?"

"Isn't it better than going back to Roehampton?"

"Oh, my dearest," she cried, bursting into tears.

He comforted her with sweet words, and even put on an air of gaiety.

"Why, my dear mother, a couple of years knocking about in Central Africa is no more nowadays than the grand tour was when Lord Chesterfield wrote those wonderful letters of his in the old house hard by."*

Lady Mary was fain to listen as he reasoned with her, arguing that a blow such as he had suffered was not to be got over by walking about the West End of London, or even mooning on the Italian Lakes, or hunting in Hampshire. He had to do something that would call upon his thews and sinews, and give his brain a holiday.

"I won't go alone, ma'am, if it would fret you. I know a splendid fellow who would go with me—and who knows the country. I shall have to be pretty artful to prevent his finding out that I don't know it."

He went off directly after breakfast to find his friend, and he set about his preparations for the journey with red-hot haste. He contrived to be occupied every day and almost every hour, till that sultry afternoon when he stood with his mother and Daisy Meredith in Southampton Docks, bidding them good-bye, before he and his comrade went on board the African steamer.

And then the women who loved him had to go back to the desolate house in the land of conventionalities, where one day and one year are painfully like every other day and year, and to harden their hearts against the pain of years in which they were not to see him, years of peril for him, years of constant anxiety for them. It had to be borne. Africa was better than Roehampton. Perils from savages, perils from wild beasts, from climate, from famine, were better than a mind extinguished, a death in life.

EPILOGUE

CONRAD kept his word to his mother, and in the second autumn after the parting at Southampton he was settled at Cranford, and Daisy Meredith had her first ride after a pack that belonged to her cousin, and in every individual whereof she could take a personal interest. His African wanderings had been marred by few misfortunes. A bout of fever, a camp-fire that consumed the travellers' stores, and left them in some danger of starvation, had been the worst incidents in travels that had extended from the Zambesi to the Congo. He came back to England in vigorous health, and he bore no outward signs of the disappointment that had changed the current of his life. He took kindly to the humdrum existence of the country squire, and rode hard, but not recklessly. He invited his friends to shoot with him over woods that had been carefully preserved during his absence, and he was active and cheerful, if not particularly joyous.

The freshness of youth and delight in trivial things had gone from him for ever. He read more, and thought more, spending solitary hours in his library. He interested himself in politics. He was a kind and energetic landlord, and built cottages that were ideal in healthfulness and comfort, aided in all his plans by Daisy's knowledge of peasant life, its needs and idiosyncrasies.

He looked, and seemed in manner and ideas, ten years older than in the brief summer of Irene's influence. When his mother tried to arouse his ambition, and wanted him to offer himself for his division of the county, he smiled, and begged her to be patient.

"I was seven years at Roehampton," he said, and she understood the cryptic reply.

It would take him long to forget. The cure had only begun in Africa. They would have to be patient, and bide their time.

Daisy was his right hand in most things on the estate, on the home farm, in the stables and kennels. She had all the instincts of a country-bred girl, though she had languished in a London suburb till her eighteenth year. A daring rider, a fervid lover of the animal creation, ardent in the chase but always sorry for the fox, she was never more charming than at Cranford. And that knack of being never in the way and never out of the way was itself a charm.

Lady Mary watched and wondered. Daisy was eight-and-twenty, but quite as pretty at that mature age as she had been at eighteen, prettier perhaps by the light of a developed intelligence that gave variety and sparkle to the face. She was not a Romney beauty, or a Raphael beauty, nor had she the sensuous lips and the dreaming violet eyes of a Rossetti beauty,* but she was pretty enough to be the sunshine of a good man's home, the smiling welcomer at the end of a day's toil, the sympathising wife in trouble and in joy. And she had bright and gracious manners that would ensure her popularity as the wife of a public man.

Lady Mary thought that, however long the courtship might hang fire, her son would end by discovering that Daisy was something more to him than the adopted sister, the useful friend, the good "Pal" he affected now to consider her; and as Daisy's father had been obliging enough to die while Conrad was in Africa, there was one obstacle the less to the marriage from a social point of view.

Of course, Daisy's mother was a difficulty; but that poor lady, having failed as a singing mistress, as a milliner, as a typewriter, as a crystal-gazer, and as a manicurist, would be amenable to reason, and could be pensioned, and relegated to a modest villa at Hastings or Ryde.

Conrad never uttered the name of his lost love after his return from Africa; but he could not hope to go through life without hearing of her, since Mr. Middlemore had crowned himself with glory by winning the Derby with Yorkshire Tyke, a horse of his own breeding. After an Indian honeymoon he had settled down in Yorkshire with his beautiful wife, who shone as a star in a society made up of land-owners in the neighbourhood, soldiers from York, and the men who came from afar for the big shoots. People talked of her as lovely, but with cold and unattractive manners. As a personality the jovial Middlemore was preferred to his beautiful wife.

They came to London for a short time in the season, but had no London house. They stayed at one of the smart hotels, and spent the greater part of their time at suburban race meetings and fashionable cricket or polo matches.

THE END

NOTES

1   *Whitechapel*: Working-class neighbourhood situated in East London and famous for being the location of the Jack the Ripper murders in 1888.

1   *Bermondsey*: Industrial district in South London in the nineteenth century well known for its slum along the riverside, as illustrated in Charles Dickens's *Oliver Twist* (1837).

1   *Mayfair*: Luxurious area in central London.

2   *souffre-douleur*: French for whipping boy, used here for a paid companion who is bullied.

6   *coiffée*: French for coiffured.

7   *portière*: a curtain hung in a doorway.

8   *novels were contraband*: Braddon frequently refers to debates on women's reading. Young women were advised to read conduct and etiquette books and avoid novels likely to arouse strong feelings. This is the case of Charlotte Brontë's *Jane Eyre* (1847), mentioned here, which features an unconventional heroine who denounces the Victorian double standard and women's subordinated condition. The alias that the character uses (Jane Brown) may recall Jane Eyre who uses the alias Jane Elliott; the young woman also admits that she strongly identifies the character, hence her reading of the novel overnight.

10   *Penelope*: Odysseus's wife in Homer's *Odyssey* known for keeping her suitors at bay while her husband is away by weaving a shroud and unravelling her work at night. The image highlights Lady Harling's calmness and control poles apart from the young girl's passionate nature.

11   *the waters of Marah*: Hebrew name meaning bitterness. References to the Bible often appear in association with Lady Harling who reads sermons at night to soothe her mind and who has a crucifix hung over her bed.

11   *The Scarlet Letter*: Novel by Nathaniel Hawthorne published in 1850. It relates the story of Hester Prynne, charged with adultery and who must thereafter wear a scarlet letter "A" on her breast as a sign of her sin. This is another reference to an improper heroine which fore-

shadows the revelation of the young woman's story. Her father's prohibition of the reading of Hawthorne's novel recalls once again the current debates on types of reading for women.

12   *haute noblesse*: French for the nobility. Many references to the aristocracy are associated with Lady Harling throughout the novel; the numerous historical references that may be traced are also meant to reinforce Lady Harling's social class.

17   *Haidee and Juan*: In Lord Byron's epic poem *Don Juan* (1819-24), Don Juan is found after his shipwreck by the daughter of a Greek pirate, Haidee. The literary intertext emphasizes once again the construction of the young woman as a romantic character. It reappears several times later on in the novel.

19   *He pardoned the nameless woman who had sinned, and saved her from the Pharisees' fierce law*: John 8:1-11. Reference to the adulterous woman whom Jesus saved from being stoned by the Pharisees. The numerous hints at adultery are designed to shape the young woman as a fallen creature.

22   *tout potage*: French for in total.

22   *Harley Street*: Famous for its medical professionals, notably the surgeon Sir Frederick Treves (1853-1923), known for his friendship with Joseph Merrick, the "Elephant Man."

23   *Absalom*: David's third son, considered the most handsome man in the kingdom.

23   *"the observed of all observers, the glass of fashion and the mould of form"*: *Hamlet* (III, 1). Ophelia's words bemoaning Hamlet's apparent madness.

23   *that famous Charles Townshend described by Walpole*: Charles Townshend (1674-1738), British Whig statesman, was Sir Robert Walpole's brother-in-law; both were in power during the reigns of George I and George II but had serious differences of opinion.

24   *Frith's picture, "Coming of age in ye olden time"*: *Coming of Age in the Olden Time* (1849), by William Powell Frith (1819-1909), English painter known for his scenes of Victorian life.

26   *the tragedy of Actæon*: In Greek mythology Actæon was changed into a stag by Artemis whom he had seen bathing in the woods and torn into pieces by his hounds.

40   *"should never know the restraints that other mental sufferers know"*: Allusion to the brutal methods used to treat insane patients before the mid-nineteenth century. In the course of the nineteenth century, alienists like John Conolly (1794-1866) helped the opening of madhouses (such as the Middlesex County Asylum at Hanwell) that sup-

ported non-restraint management, as expounded in his *The Treatment of the Insane Without Mechanical Restraints* (1856).

44 *the books, Darwin, Wallace, Tyndall, Clodd, and several new books on electricity*: Charles Darwin (1809-1882), Alfred Russel Wallace (1823-1913), John Tyndall (1820-1893), Edward Clodd (1840-1930). The naturalists Darwin and Wallace, the physicist Tyndall and the anthropologist Clodd represent modern science and new theorizations on the natural world that developed and were popularised in the second half of the nineteenth century.

45 *preux chevalier*: French for valiant knight. The term highlights Conrad's noble social background as much as his romantic character.

47 *"The earth and every common sight"*: Reference to William Wordsworth's "Ode: Intimations of Immortality from Recollections of Early Childhood." The poem deals with childhood memories and compares life with "a sleep and a forgetting" (l. 59), matching Conrad's memory troubles and the "slumber" of his brain.

47 *Barbarossa's cavern*: the legend says that Frederick I Barbarossa will remain sleeping in an underground palace in Bavaria until Germany is unified.

48 *From the Congo ... on the Nyanza*: References to African exploration in the second half of the nineteenth century. Zanzibar (which is now part of Tanzania) is where the missionary David Livingstone (1813-1873) returned in 1866 to seek the source of the Nile. English explorers are mentioned later on, many of them looking for the source of the Nile, such as Samuel White Baker (1821-1893), whose bestseller *The Albert N'Yanza* (1866) contributed to the popularisation of African exploration.

50 *a cheap Alcides*: Heracles (or Hercules for the Romans), Greek hero famous for his strength and courage.

55 *than Peter Bell had about a primrose by the river's brim*: William Wordsworth's "Peter Bell: A Tale in Verse" (1798). The poem relates the story of Peter Bell who is immune to the influence of nature until he encounters a dead man and his grieving family.

58 *Livingstone*: The missionary David Livingstone (1813-1873) who explored southeastern Africa. His journal, *Missionary Travels and Researches in South Africa*, was published in 1857.

58 *With Stanley, with Cameron, with Burton, with Trivier*: Henry Morton Stanley (1844-1904), Verney Lovett Cameron (1844-1894), Richard Francis Burton (1821-1890) and Elisée Trivier (1842-1912), were explorers of Africa whose journeys were popularised in the last decades of

the nineteenth century, as in Cameron's *Across Africa* (1877) and *To the Gold Coast for Gold* (1883), Stanley's bestseller *How I Found Livingstone* (1872) and *In Darkest Africa* (1890) or Burton's *The Lake Regions of Central Africa: A Picture of Exploration* (1860) and *Wanderings in West Africa, from Liverpool to Fernando Po* (1863).

61   *ortolans*: Birds generally roasted and eaten whole as a delicacy.

62   *West African row*: Possible reference to the Benin expedition of 1897.

63   *rest-cure girls*: This is a possible ironic reference to the treatment for nervous illness conceived by the American neurologist Silas Weir Mitchell (1829-1914) whose rest cure consisted in enforcing bed rest. The patients were not allowed to read, however, nor carry out any kind of intellectual activity. What is interesting here is that Mitchell treated men and women alike and was particularly involved with wounded soldiers during the Civil War. His interest in and work on nervous men, and more particularly war veterans, may explain Braddon's hint since her novel illuminates modern constructions of mental diseases and the emergence of medical discourses on trauma.

65   *bonbonnière*: chocolate-box house.

66   *Burma*: the third Anglo-Burmese war took place in November 1885. The province of Burma in British India became a major province in 1897.

66   *Waziristan*: There were several British expeditions led in Waziristan around the turn of the century, especially in 1894, 1897 and 1902. It is likely that Sir Michael Thelliston participated in the 1894 expedition then left for West Africa to participate in the Benin expedition of 1897.

66   *K.C.B.*: Knight Commander of the Order of the Bath, second level of the Order of the Bath, a British order of chivalry.

67   *Tom Moore's lovely song "Full many a gem of purest ray"*: Reference to Thomas Moore (1779-1852), romantic Irish poet whose songs were very popular. "Full many a gem of purest ray" is a verse from Thomas Gray's masterpiece, "Elegy in a Country Churchyard", published in 1751, which was oftentimes plagiarised.

67   *Chars-à-bancs*: horse-drawn carriage.

69   *"too rash, too unadvised, too sudden, / Too like the lightning, which doth cease to be / Ere one can say it lightens?"*: Citation from Shakespeare's *Romeo and Juliet* (II, ii). The manifold references to Shakespeare's tragedy throughout the novel doom the relationship between Irene and Conrad.

70   *in formâ pauperis*: Latin legal phrase meaning "in the form of a pauper" allowing non-payment of costs for a criminal defence.

71   *a Leighton, a Poynter, a Frank Dicksee, two classical subjects by Albert Moore, a dog and a girl by Briton Rivière, and an Alma Tadema*: Sir Frederic Leighton (1830-1896), Sir Edward John Poynter (1836-1919), Sir Frank Bernard Dicksee (1853-1928), Albert Joseph Moore (1841-1893), Briton Rivière (1840-1920), Sir Lawrence Alma-Tadema (1836-1912), British painters most of all known for their sensuous female characters. Several of Briton Rivière's works feature a girl and a dog.

73   *what Nature did for Wordsworth's Lucy*: Reference to the Lucy poems by William Wordsworth, a series of five poems composed between 1798 and 1801 and dealing with an idealised English girl, her relationship with nature and her premature death. The romantic intertext may once again be read as an ominous motif.

74   *dans le temps*: French for in her youth.

74   *the Burlington Arcade*: Fashionable shopping gallery in the nineteenth century.

74   *hare's foot*: used to apply powder.

86   *hamadryad*: tree nymph.

86   *au fond*: French for actually.

87   *"He never loved that loved not at first sight"*: "Who ever loved that loved not at first sight?" Citation from Shakespeare's *As You Like It* (III, v).

89   *a Ruskinesque effect*: The reference to John Ruskin (1819-1900), who was a critic of art and architecture, points out the architect's Gothic style. Ruskin played a key part in the development of the aesthetics of Romanticism. It is not surprising here that the romantic Irene likes the architect's stone-mullioned, mediæval windows while Lady Harling prefers the original arrangement of the house.

91   *Lawrence to Buckner*: Thomas Lawrence (1769-1830) and Richard Buckner (1812-1883), English portrait painters.

91   *felucca*: Small vessel especially used on the Nile and more widely in the Mediterranean region.

95   *the Grenadiers*: The Grenadier Guards is an infantry regiment of the British army. It took part in the Anglo-Egyptian War of 1882 and was involved in the Boer Wars.

98   *landau*: Horse-drawn four-wheeled carriage.

115   *like Lady Hamilton in Romney's pictures*: Lady Hamilton (1765-1815) was the muse of the painter George Romney (1734-1802) and she was famous for her affair with Lord Nelson. This is another refer-

ence which lets Irene's sensuality transpire and constructs her as
an adulteress. Lady Hamilton's loose-fitting garments on many of
Romney's pictures recall the first depiction of Irene Thelliston on
board the *Electra*.

124 *black as Erebus*: In Greek mythology Erebus is the personification of
darkness.

129 *Jephthah's daughter*: In the Old Testament Jephthah sacrificed his
daughter after swearing that "whatsoever cometh forth of the doors
of my house to meet me, when I return in peace from the children
of Ammon, shall surely be the Lord's, and I will offer it up for a burnt
offering" (Judges 11:31). The biblical reference clearly constructs
Irene as a victim.

131 *Central Africa is no more nowadays than the grand tour was when Lord
Chesterfield wrote those wonderful letters of his in the old house hard by*:
Reference to the letters that Philip Stanhope, 4th Earl of Chesterfield (1694-1773) wrote to his son, some of them providing advice
concerning how to behave while on a Grand Tour. A collection of
the letters was published in 1774.

133 *the dreaming violet eyes of a Rossetti beauty*: Dante Gabriel Rossetti
(1828-1882), English poet and painter who founded the Pre-Raphaelite Brotherhood in 1848 with William Holman Hunt (1827-1910)
and John Everett Millais (1829-1896). Rossetti was known to work
with three female models, Elizabeth Siddal, Fanny Cornforth and
Jane Morris. The latter particularly embodied the Pre-Raphaelite
ideal of beauty.